# Thoughtbound Guardians

**Thoughtbound, Volume 3**

Tori Honda

Published by Tori Honda, 2024.

This is a work of fiction. Similarities to real people, places, or events are entirely coincidental.

THOUGHTBOUND GUARDIANS

**First edition. December 10, 2024.**



ISBN: 979-8230063339

Written by Tori Honda.

Thoughtboud:Guardians

**Prologue: Shadows Rising**

As I stood at the edge of the forest, the air around me felt heavy with anticipation. The sun had long since set, casting the land in a cloak of darkness, and the only light came from the faint glow of the moon and stars above. I could sense the change in the atmosphere, the subtle shift that hinted at a brewing storm. The shadows seemed to dance and writhe, as if alive with malevolent intent.

The vision had come to me in a dream—a vivid and unsettling glimpse into the future. I saw the Shadow Lord, a figure of terrifying power and malevolence, gathering his forces for the ultimate battle against the light. His presence loomed large, casting a pall over the land, and I knew that our greatest challenge lay ahead.

In the vision, I saw our home, Ravenswood, and the neighboring village of Blackwood, standing as beacons of hope and resilience. But they were surrounded by an encroaching darkness, a tide of shadow that threatened to consume everything we held dear. I saw the faces of those I loved—Daniel, Clara, Lucas, Elara, and Alaric—each one filled with determination and resolve. We had fought so hard to protect our home, and now, we faced our greatest test.

The Shadow Lord's army was vast, a legion of dark creatures and twisted beings, each one more terrifying than the last. They moved with purpose, driven by their master's will, and I knew that we had to be prepared for the onslaught. The vision showed me glimpses of the battles to come, the fierce clashes of light and darkness, and the sacrifices that would be required.

But amidst the chaos and uncertainty, there was a glimmer of hope. I saw a hidden power within me, a force that could tip the balance in our favor. The ancient prophecy that Lucas had discovered spoke of a chosen one, a guardian of the light who would lead us to victory. I realized that this power was within me, waiting to be unlocked, and it filled me with a renewed sense of purpose.

As the vision faded, I was left with a profound sense of responsibility. The fate of our world hung in the balance, and it was up to us to protect it. I turned away from the forest, my heart heavy with the knowledge of what lay ahead, but also filled with determination. We would face the darkness together, and we would not falter.

Returning to Ravenswood, I found my friends waiting for me. Their faces were etched with concern, but their eyes held a fierce resolve. We had come through so much together, and now, we stood on the brink of our greatest battle.

"We need to gather our allies," I said, my voice steady despite the turmoil within me. "The Shadow Lord is preparing for war, and we must be ready to face him. Our unity and strength will be our greatest weapons."

Daniel stepped forward, his expression filled with unwavering support. "We'll stand by you, Olivia. Together, we can face anything."

Clara nodded, her eyes shining with determination. "We'll gather our forces and prepare for the battles ahead. The light within us will guide us through the darkness."

Lucas and Elara exchanged a resolute glance, while Alaric's presence radiated strength and confidence. We were a team, united by our shared purpose and the bonds we had forged through countless trials.

As we prepared for the challenges ahead, I couldn't help but feel a sense of anticipation. The final battle between light and darkness was drawing near, and we were ready to face it head-on. With the strength and resilience of our community, and the power within me waiting to be unleashed, we would stand against the Shadow Lord and protect our world.

That night, as the moon rose high in the sky, casting its gentle light over Ravenswood, I made a silent vow. We would continue to stand against the darkness, no matter the cost. With our unity and determination, we would face whatever challenges lay ahead and build a future filled with promise and possibility.

THIS PROLOGUE SETS the stage for the epic conclusion of the trilogy, from Olivia's perspective, highlighting the impending threat of the Shadow Lord and the determination of the Guardians to stand against the darkness. Let me know if you'd like to continue with the next chapter or if there are any adjustments you'd like to make!

### **Chapter 1: Gathering the Allies**

The morning sun cast a warm, golden light over Ravenswood as we prepared to set out on our journey. The air was crisp, and the village was bustling with activity as everyone worked together to strengthen our defenses and make final preparations. Our goal was clear: gather allies and form a united front against the Shadow Lord.

As we assembled in the town square, I felt a mixture of determination and anticipation. Beside me stood Daniel, Clara, Lucas, Elara, and Alaric—each one ready to face whatever challenges lay ahead. The bond between us was strong, forged through countless trials, and I knew we would need every ounce of that strength in the days to come.

"We need to visit the neighboring villages and towns," Clara said, her voice filled with purpose. "We must convince them to join us in this fight. Their support will be crucial in the battle against the Shadow Lord."

Lucas nodded in agreement. "The ancient texts speak of the importance of unity. We must come together if we are to stand a chance."

Elara, ever the strategist, added, "I'll coordinate with our scouts to ensure that we can reach as many communities as possible. We need to move quickly and efficiently."

Alaric, his presence radiating confidence, said, "I'll lead the way. My knowledge of the terrain and combat skills will be useful in navigating any obstacles we may encounter."

Daniel, standing beside me, placed a reassuring hand on my shoulder. "We'll face this together, Olivia. Our bond is strong, and we can handle anything."

I felt a surge of determination. "Let's do this. We'll protect our home and build a future filled with promise and possibility."

OUR FIRST STOP WAS the village of Eldor, where we hoped to rally the support of their skilled warriors and wise leaders. The journey through the forest was filled with a sense of urgency, and we moved swiftly, our senses heightened by the ever-present threat of dark forces.

As we approached Eldor, we were greeted by the village leader, a stern but kind-hearted woman named Hilda. Her expression was one of concern, but also of determination.

"Welcome, Guardians," Hilda said, her voice steady. "We have heard of your bravery and the battles you have faced. What brings you to Eldor?"

Clara stepped forward, her expression resolute. "Hilda, we need your help. The Shadow Lord is preparing for war, and we must unite to stand against him. Your warriors and knowledge will be invaluable in the fight to come."

Hilda listened intently, her eyes filled with a mixture of worry and resolve. "The Shadow Lord's forces have already caused trouble in our lands. We will stand with you, Guardians. Our strength lies in our unity."

With Eldor's support secured, we continued our journey, visiting neighboring villages and towns to rally more allies. Each community welcomed us with a mixture of admiration and determination, ready to stand together in the face of the impending darkness.

AS THE DAYS PASSED, our coalition grew stronger. Leaders and warriors from across the land joined our cause, bringing with them their unique skills and knowledge. The sense of unity and purpose was palpable, and I felt a renewed sense of hope.

One evening, as the sun set and cast a warm golden light over the camp, we gathered to discuss our progress and plan our next steps. The atmosphere was charged with anticipation and resolve.

"We have made great strides in gathering our allies," Clara said, her voice filled with pride. "But we must remain vigilant. The Shadow Lord's forces are growing stronger, and we must be prepared for anything."

Lucas nodded, his expression serious. "The ancient prophecy speaks of a chosen one who will lead us to victory. We must uncover the full meaning of this prophecy and unlock Olivia's true potential."

Elara, ever the strategist, added, "I'll continue to coordinate our efforts and ensure that our defenses are impenetrable. Our unity and determination will be our greatest strengths."

Daniel, standing beside me, placed a reassuring hand on my shoulder. "We'll face this together, Olivia. Our bond is strong, and we can handle anything."

I felt a surge of determination. "Let's do this. We'll protect our home and build a future filled with promise and possibility."

As we prepared for the challenges ahead, the sense of unity and resolve within our coalition grew stronger. We knew that the final battle between light and darkness was approaching, and we were ready to face it together.

That night, as the moon rose high in the sky, casting its gentle light over the camp, I made a silent vow. We would continue to stand against the darkness, no matter the cost. With the strength and resilience of our community, and the deepening bond between us, we would face

whatever challenges lay ahead and build a future filled with promise and possibility.

### **CHAPTER 2: THE ANCIENT Prophecy**

The coalition we had formed was growing stronger with each passing day, but there was an undercurrent of urgency that none of us could ignore. The Shadow Lord's forces were preparing for war, and time was of the essence. We needed to uncover every possible advantage we could find, and that meant delving deeper into the ancient prophecy Lucas had uncovered.

One crisp morning, as the sun cast its warm light over the camp, Lucas called for an urgent meeting. His expression was one of excitement and determination, and I knew he had made an important discovery.

"Everyone," Lucas began, his voice filled with purpose, "I have found more information about the ancient prophecy. It speaks of a chosen one who will lead us to victory against the Shadow Lord. This prophecy holds the key to unlocking Olivia's true potential."

The room fell silent as we listened intently to Lucas's words. The weight of the prophecy settled over us, and I felt a mixture of anticipation and responsibility.

"The prophecy mentions a hidden power within Olivia," Lucas continued, his eyes locking onto mine. "This power is tied to the Guardians of old and can only be unlocked through a series of trials. We must find these trials and complete them to unlock Olivia's true potential."

Clara's expression grew serious. "Where do we begin, Lucas? How do we find these trials?"

Lucas unfurled an ancient map he had been studying. "The map points to a series of locations scattered across the land. Each location holds a trial designed to test strength, unity, and resolve. We must journey to these places and face the challenges they present."

Elara, ever the strategist, added, "We need to approach this carefully. The trials will not be easy, and the Shadow Lord's forces may try to stop us. We must stay together and move quickly."

Alaric, his presence radiating confidence, said, "I'll lead the way. My knowledge of the terrain and combat skills will be useful in navigating any obstacles we may encounter."

Daniel, standing beside me, placed a reassuring hand on my shoulder. "We'll face this together, Olivia. Our bond is strong, and we can handle anything."

I felt a surge of determination. "Let's do this. We'll uncover the secrets of the prophecy and unlock my true potential."

OUR FIRST DESTINATION was an ancient ruin hidden deep within the forest. The journey was filled with a sense of anticipation and purpose as we made our way through the dense foliage. The air was cool, and the sounds of nature provided a soothing backdrop to our thoughts.

As we approached the ruins, the sight was awe-inspiring. The ancient structures were covered in intricate carvings and symbols, each one telling a story of the Guardians who had come before us.

"This is it," Lucas said, his voice filled with reverence. "The first trial awaits us within these ruins."

Clara cautioned, "We must be prepared for anything. The trials will test us in ways we cannot anticipate."

Alaric led the way, his eyes scanning the surroundings for any signs of danger. As we entered the ruins, the air grew cooler, and the light from the carvings seemed to grow stronger. The walls were lined with ancient relics and artifacts, each one holding a piece of history and knowledge.

We soon came upon a large chamber with a series of intricate puzzles and mechanisms built into the walls. "These puzzles must be the key to unlocking the trial," I said, my voice filled with determination. "We need to solve them to proceed."

With careful coordination, we worked together to solve the puzzles. Each mechanism required a combination of our skills and knowledge, and I could feel the bond between us growing stronger with each successful step.

Finally, the last puzzle clicked into place, and a hidden door slowly creaked open. The chamber beyond was filled with an ethereal light, and at its center stood an ancient pedestal with a glowing artifact.

"This artifact," Lucas said, his voice filled with awe, "it holds the power of the first trial. Olivia, you must harness its energy."

I approached the pedestal, my heart pounding with anticipation. As I reached out to touch the artifact, a surge of energy flowed through me, filling me with a sense of strength and clarity.

The trial had begun.

### **CHAPTER 3: TRIALS and Tribulations**

The glowing artifact's energy surged through me, filling me with a newfound sense of strength and clarity. The first trial had begun, and I could feel the power of the Guardians coursing through my veins. As I stood at the center of the chamber, surrounded by the ethereal light, I knew that this was just the beginning of our journey.

My friends stood around me, their expressions filled with anticipation and determination. Clara stepped forward, her voice steady. "Olivia, this is your trial, but we are here to support you. The prophecy speaks of unity and strength, and we will face these challenges together."

Lucas nodded, his eyes filled with awe. "The artifact holds the power of the first trial. We must harness its energy and complete the challenges it presents."

Elara, ever the strategist, added, "We'll need to stay vigilant and work together. The trials will test us in ways we cannot anticipate."

Alaric, his presence radiating confidence, said, "I'll be ready for any obstacles we may encounter. Together, we can overcome anything."

Daniel, standing beside me, placed a reassuring hand on my shoulder. "We're with you, Olivia. Our bond is strong, and we can handle anything."

I took a deep breath, feeling the support of my friends. "Let's do this. We'll face these trials together and unlock my true potential."

THE FIRST TRIAL BEGAN with a test of strength and endurance. The chamber transformed, and we found ourselves in a vast, rocky landscape. The air was thick with heat, and the ground beneath our feet was uneven and treacherous.

"We need to navigate this terrain and reach the other side," Clara said, her voice filled with determination. "This trial will test our physical strength and endurance."

Alaric took the lead, his combat skills and knowledge of the terrain proving invaluable. We moved quickly and carefully, navigating the rocky landscape with precision. The heat was intense, and our muscles ached with the effort, but we pushed forward, our determination unwavering.

As we made our way through the landscape, we encountered a series of obstacles designed to test our agility and teamwork. Giant boulders blocked our path, and narrow ledges required us to balance with precision. Each obstacle required a combination of our skills and coordination, and I could feel the bond between us growing stronger with each successful step.

Finally, we reached the other side of the landscape, where a shimmering portal awaited us. The first trial was complete, and I could feel the energy of the artifact growing stronger.

THE SECOND TRIAL WAS a test of wisdom and intellect. The chamber transformed once more, and we found ourselves in a grand library filled with ancient tomes and scrolls. The air was cool and filled with the scent of old books and parchment.

Lucas's eyes lit up with curiosity. "This trial will test our knowledge and problem-solving skills. We must decipher the ancient texts and solve the puzzles they present."

We spread out through the library, each of us focusing on different sections of the ancient texts. The puzzles were intricate and complex, requiring us to use our intellect and intuition to uncover their secrets. As we worked together, I could feel the bond between us growing stronger, our minds and hearts united in the pursuit of knowledge.

After hours of intense concentration and collaboration, we deciphered the final puzzle. A hidden door slowly creaked open, revealing a second artifact glowing with an ethereal light. The second trial was complete, and I could feel my connection to the Guardians deepening.

THE THIRD TRIAL WAS a test of courage and resolve. The chamber transformed once more, and we found ourselves in a dark, foreboding forest. The air was thick with an oppressive energy, and the shadows seemed to come to life around us.

Elara's expression grew serious. "This trial will test our courage and resolve. We must navigate this forest and face the fears that lie within."

As we made our way through the forest, the oppressive energy grew stronger. Dark creatures and twisted beings emerged from the shadows, their eyes gleaming with malevolent intent. We faced them with courage and determination, our unity and strength guiding us through the darkness.

Each step forward was a test of our resolve, but we pressed on, our bond growing stronger with each challenge we overcame. Finally, we reached the heart of the forest, where a third artifact awaited us, glowing with an otherworldly light. The third trial was complete, and I could feel the full potential of my abilities beginning to awaken.

AS WE EMERGED FROM the forest, the sense of accomplishment and hope was palpable. We had faced the trials and emerged stronger, our unity and determination guiding us through each challenge. The artifacts we had collected pulsed with powerful energy, and I knew that we were ready to face whatever lay ahead.

That night, as the moon rose high in the sky, casting its gentle light over the camp, I made a silent vow. We would continue to stand against the darkness, no matter the cost. With the strength and resilience of our community, and the deepening bond between us, we would face whatever challenges lay ahead and build a future filled with promise and possibility.

### **CHAPTER 4: THE HIDDEN Sanctuary**

Having successfully completed the first three trials, we felt a renewed sense of strength and unity. The artifacts we had collected pulsed with powerful energy, and I could feel my connection to the Guardians deepening. Our next destination, according to Lucas's research, was the hidden sanctuary where the Guardians of old once trained and prepared for battle. This sanctuary was said to hold the final pieces of the puzzle that would unlock my true potential.

The journey to the hidden sanctuary took us through dense forests, across rugged mountains, and along ancient paths that had long been forgotten. The air was filled with a sense of anticipation and purpose as we navigated the treacherous terrain. Alaric's knowledge of the landscape and his combat skills proved invaluable, guiding us safely through each obstacle we encountered.

As we approached the sanctuary, the sight before us was awe-inspiring. The ancient structure was nestled within a hidden valley, its walls covered in intricate carvings and symbols that seemed to radiate a faint, otherworldly light. The sanctuary exuded an aura of wisdom and power, and I could feel the presence of the Guardians who had come before us.

"This is it," Clara said, her voice filled with reverence. "The hidden sanctuary of the Guardians. We must be prepared for the challenges that lie within."

Lucas examined the carvings on the walls, his eyes filled with awe. "The symbols tell the story of the Guardians who trained here, each one unlocking their true potential through trials of strength, wisdom, and courage. We are following in their footsteps."

Elara, ever the strategist, added, "We need to approach this carefully. The sanctuary may hold powerful enchantments and trials that will test us to our limits. We must stay together and move with caution."

Daniel, standing beside me, placed a reassuring hand on my shoulder. "We'll face this together, Olivia. Our bond is strong, and we can handle anything."

I took a deep breath, feeling the support of my friends. "Let's do this. We'll unlock the secrets of the sanctuary and uncover my true potential."

AS WE ENTERED THE SANCTUARY, the air grew cooler, and the light from the carvings seemed to grow stronger. The walls were lined with ancient relics and artifacts, each one holding a piece of history and knowledge. We moved cautiously, our senses heightened by the presence of powerful magic.

The first chamber we entered was filled with intricate mechanisms and puzzles, similar to those we had encountered in the trials. "These puzzles are designed to test our intellect and problem-solving skills," Lucas said, his voice filled with determination. "We must work together to solve them."

With careful coordination, we began to decipher the puzzles. Each mechanism required a combination of our skills and knowledge, and I could feel the bond between us growing stronger with each successful step. The challenges tested our patience and ingenuity, but we pressed on, determined to unlock the secrets of the sanctuary.

After hours of intense concentration, the final puzzle clicked into place, and a hidden door slowly creaked open. The chamber beyond was filled with an ethereal light, and at its center stood an ancient pedestal with a glowing artifact.

"This artifact holds the power of the Guardians," Lucas said, his voice filled with awe. "Olivia, you must harness its energy."

As I approached the pedestal, a surge of energy flowed through me, filling me with a sense of strength and clarity. I could feel the presence of the Guardians, guiding and supporting me. The artifact's energy connected with the other artifacts we had collected, creating a powerful resonance that deepened my connection to the Guardians.

THE NEXT CHAMBER WE entered was a vast training hall, filled with ancient weapons and combat dummies. The air was thick with the remnants of powerful enchantments, and I could sense the presence of the Guardians who had trained here.

"This hall is where the Guardians honed their combat skills," Alaric said, his voice filled with respect. "We must face these challenges and prove our strength and resolve."

As we trained together, I could feel my combat skills improving. Each session was a test of our strength, agility, and coordination. We sparred with each other, honed our techniques, and pushed ourselves to our limits. The bond between us grew stronger with each challenge we overcame.

THE FINAL CHAMBER WE entered was a grand hall filled with ancient texts and scrolls. The air was cool and filled with the scent of old parchment. This hall was the heart of the sanctuary, where the Guardians had studied and meditated to unlock their true potential.

Lucas examined the texts, his eyes filled with awe. "These texts hold the wisdom of the Guardians. We must study them and understand their teachings."

We spread out through the hall, each of us focusing on different sections of the ancient texts. The wisdom contained within the pages was profound, and I could feel my understanding of light and darkness deepening. The teachings of the Guardians resonated with me, guiding me on my journey to unlock my true potential.

After hours of intense study and meditation, I felt a surge of energy and clarity. The power of the Guardians was now fully awakened within me, and I knew that we were ready to face whatever challenges lay ahead.

AS WE EMERGED FROM the sanctuary, the sense of accomplishment and hope was palpable. We had unlocked the secrets of the Guardians and strengthened our bond. The artifacts we had collected pulsed with powerful energy, and I knew that we were ready to face the Shadow Lord and protect our world.

That night, as the moon rose high in the sky, casting its gentle light over the camp, I made a silent vow. We would continue to stand against the darkness, no matter the cost. With the strength and resilience of our community, and the deepening bond between us, we would face whatever challenges lay ahead and build a future filled with promise and possibility.

### **CHAPTER 6: THE BATTLE Begins**

The final leg of our journey was marked by an increasing sense of urgency and resolve. We knew that the Shadow Lord's stronghold lay just ahead, and the fate of our world depended on the outcome of the impending battle. Our forces moved with purpose, their unity and determination palpable. The air was thick with tension, and every step brought us closer to the ultimate confrontation.

As we approached the stronghold, the landscape grew darker and more foreboding. The oppressive energy that permeated the air was almost tangible, and the sight of the Shadow Lord's fortress sent shivers down my spine. The dark, towering structure loomed ahead, its walls lined with twisted, malevolent beings ready to defend their master.

We set up camp a short distance from the stronghold, using the cover of the forest to conceal our presence. The leaders of our coalition gathered in a makeshift command tent to discuss our strategy. The atmosphere was charged with anticipation and resolve.

Clara addressed the group, her voice steady and authoritative. "We are standing on the brink of the final battle. Our unity and strength will guide us through the challenges ahead. We must be prepared for anything and trust in each other."

Lucas nodded in agreement. "The knowledge and power we have gained from the Guardians will be our greatest weapons. We must use them wisely and protect the light within us."

Elara, ever the strategist, added, "We need to coordinate our efforts and ensure that our defenses are impenetrable. The Shadow Lord's forces are powerful, but our unity will make us stronger."

Alaric, his presence radiating confidence, said, "I'll lead the charge. My knowledge of combat and strategy will be invaluable in navigating the obstacles we may encounter."

Daniel, standing beside me, placed a reassuring hand on my shoulder. "We'll face this together, Olivia. Our bond is strong, and we can handle anything."

I felt a surge of determination. "Let's do this. We'll face the Shadow Lord and protect our home."

AS DAWN BROKE, CASTING a faint light over the landscape, our forces prepared for battle. The air was filled with a sense of anticipation and resolve. The time had come to face the darkness head-on.

Our archers took their positions, their bows ready to rain down arrows upon the enemy. Our warriors formed ranks, their weapons gleaming in the early light. The mages and healers stood ready to support and protect, their spells and abilities a crucial part of our strategy.

With a coordinated signal, our forces advanced toward the stronghold. The ground trembled with the sound of marching feet, and the clash of steel rang through the air as we engaged the Shadow Lord's minions. The battle was intense and chaotic, the clash of light and darkness echoing across the landscape.

Our unity and determination guided us through the fray. Alaric led the charge, his combat skills and strategic mind proving invaluable. Clara and Lucas coordinated our efforts, their leadership ensuring that we moved as one cohesive unit. Elara's strategic insights helped us navigate the battlefield, turning obstacles into opportunities. Daniel fought by my side, his presence a constant source of support and strength.

As we pressed forward, I felt the power of the Guardians surging within me. Drawing upon the energy of the artifacts we had collected, I channeled brilliant beams of light that cut through the darkness, creating openings in the Shadow Lord's defenses. My friends and allies rallied around me, their strength and resolve guiding us through the battle.

AFTER HOURS OF FIERCE combat, we reached the outer walls of the stronghold. The dark forces that had once seemed insurmountable were now faltering under the combined might of our coalition. But we knew that the greatest challenge still lay ahead.

With renewed determination, we breached the stronghold's defenses and entered the dark, twisted corridors within. The air was thick with malevolent energy, and the shadows seemed to come to life around us. But our unity and the power of the Guardians guided us through each step.

As we made our way deeper into the stronghold, we encountered powerful guardians and traps designed to deter us. Each challenge tested our strength and resolve, but we pressed on, our bond growing stronger with each obstacle we overcame.

Finally, we reached the inner sanctum of the Shadow Lord's stronghold. The chamber was filled with an oppressive darkness, and at its center stood the Shadow Lord himself. His presence radiated malevolence and power, and I could feel the weight of his gaze upon us.

"We have come to end your reign of terror, Shadow Lord," I said, my voice steady and filled with resolve. "Your darkness will not prevail."

The Shadow Lord's eyes gleamed with malevolent intent. "You are brave to come here, Guardians. But your light is no match for my power. You will fall, and darkness will consume your world."

The final battle had begun.

### **CHAPTER 7: THE FINAL Confrontation**

The air in the inner sanctum was thick with tension and dark energy. The Shadow Lord stood before us, his presence radiating malevolence and power. His eyes gleamed with a terrifying intent, and the oppressive darkness seemed to pulse in rhythm with his heartbeat. This was the moment we had prepared for, the culmination of all our trials and sacrifices. We stood united, ready to face the ultimate challenge and protect our world from the impending darkness.

Daniel, Clara, Lucas, Elara, Alaric, and I formed a resolute line, our unity and determination palpable. The artifacts we had collected glowed with a powerful light, their energy resonating within us. The final battle had begun.

With a wave of his hand, the Shadow Lord unleashed a torrent of dark energy that surged towards us. We responded in unison, raising our weapons and channeling the power of the Guardians. A brilliant shield of light formed around us, deflecting the dark energy and illuminating the chamber with its radiance.

Clara's voice rang out, steady and commanding. "Stay together! Our unity is our greatest strength. We can defeat him if we fight as one!"

Lucas and Elara moved to flank the Shadow Lord, their coordinated attacks striking with precision. Alaric led the charge, his combat skills and strategic mind proving invaluable. Daniel fought by my side, his presence a constant source of support and strength.

The Shadow Lord moved with an unnatural speed and agility, his attacks relentless and powerful. Each clash of light and darkness sent shockwaves through the chamber, the air crackling with energy. The battle tested our limits, but we pressed on, our resolve unshaken.

As I channeled the power of the artifacts, I felt a surge of energy and clarity. The Guardians' presence was strong within me, guiding my actions and strengthening my resolve. Drawing upon their wisdom and strength, I launched a series of powerful attacks that pierced through the darkness, striking the Shadow Lord with precision.

But the Shadow Lord was not easily defeated. With a roar of rage, he summoned a vortex of dark energy that threatened to engulf us. The chamber trembled with the force of his power, and the oppressive darkness grew thicker.

"We need to disrupt his control over the dark energy!" Lucas called out, his voice filled with determination. "If we can weaken his connection, we can turn the tide of the battle."

Elara's eyes gleamed with understanding. "Olivia, focus on the artifacts! Channel their energy to disrupt the Shadow Lord's control. We'll protect you while you do."

With a nod of determination, I closed my eyes and focused on the glowing artifacts. Their energy pulsed through me, connecting me to the power of the Guardians. I could feel the ancient wisdom and strength guiding me, their light pushing back against the darkness.

As I channeled the energy, a brilliant beam of light erupted from the artifacts, piercing through the vortex of dark energy. The Shadow Lord staggered, his connection to the darkness weakening. My friends and allies rallied around me, their combined strength overwhelming the Shadow Lord's defenses.

But the Shadow Lord was not yet defeated. With a final, desperate effort, he unleashed a powerful wave of dark energy that sent us sprawling. The chamber shook with the force of his attack, and the oppressive darkness seemed to close in around us.

I struggled to my feet, my body aching from the impact. The Shadow Lord stood before me, his form flickering with malevolent energy. I could feel the weight of his gaze upon me, and I knew that the final confrontation had come.

"You cannot defeat me, Guardian," the Shadow Lord hissed, his voice filled with malice. "The darkness is eternal. Your light will falter, and I will consume your world."

With a surge of determination, I drew upon the power of the artifacts one final time. The energy of the Guardians surged through me, filling me with strength and clarity. I could feel their presence, their light pushing back against the darkness.

"No," I said, my voice steady and unwavering. "The light within us is stronger than any darkness. We will stand against you, no matter the cost."

With a final, decisive effort, I channeled all of my energy into a brilliant beam of light that struck the Shadow Lord. The chamber was filled with a blinding radiance, the darkness pushed back by the overwhelming power of the Guardians.

The Shadow Lord screamed in rage and despair, his form disintegrating into a cloud of dark energy. The oppressive darkness that had once filled the chamber was replaced by a soothing, radiant light. The final confrontation was over, and the Shadow Lord had been defeated.

As the light faded, I felt a sense of relief and triumph wash over me. My friends and allies stood by my side, their expressions filled with pride and gratitude. We had faced the darkness and emerged victorious, our unity and determination guiding us through the ultimate challenge.

That night, as the moon rose high in the sky, casting its gentle light over the stronghold, I made a silent vow. We would continue to protect our world, no matter the cost. With the strength and resilience of our community, and the deepening bond between us, we would build a future filled with promise and possibility.

### **Chapter 8: The Sacrifice**

The victory over the Shadow Lord came at a great cost. The battle had tested our limits, pushing us to the brink of our strength and resolve. As the darkness faded and the light of the Guardians filled the chamber, a profound sense of relief and triumph washed over us. But even in this moment of victory, I knew that the price we had paid was steep.

We stood together in the inner sanctum, the artifacts glowing with a radiant light. The oppressive darkness that had once filled the chamber was gone, replaced by a soothing, comforting presence. The Shadow Lord had been defeated, and the world was safe once more.

But the toll of the battle was evident. Our bodies ached with exhaustion, and the weight of the sacrifices we had made hung heavy in the air. Daniel, Clara, Lucas, Elara, Alaric, and I stood side by side, united by our shared experience and the bonds we had forged.

As we took a moment to catch our breath, the reality of what had transpired began to sink in. The power of the Guardians had been our greatest weapon, but it had also demanded a great price. The energy I had channeled to defeat the Shadow Lord had taken a toll on me, and I could feel the strain in every fiber of my being.

Daniel, ever vigilant and supportive, placed a reassuring hand on my shoulder. "Olivia, are you alright? You look...pale."

I managed a weak smile, my voice trembling with fatigue. "I'm fine, Daniel. Just...tired. The power of the Guardians...it was overwhelming."

Clara's eyes were filled with concern. "You've done so much, Olivia. You've led us through the trials, faced the Shadow Lord, and protected our world. We couldn't have done it without you."

Lucas nodded, his expression somber. "The Guardians' power is immense, but it comes at a cost. We must be mindful of that."

Elara, ever the strategist, added, "We need to ensure that the energy we've used is balanced and restored. The world must heal, just as we must."

Alaric, his presence radiating strength and confidence, said, "We will face this challenge together, just as we have faced every other. Our unity and determination will guide us through."

As we made our way back to the entrance of the stronghold, the sense of exhaustion and relief mingled with a deep gratitude for what we had achieved. The world was safe, and the darkness had been banished. But the journey was far from over.

AS WE EMERGED FROM the stronghold, the sight of our allies and friends waiting for us filled me with a renewed sense of hope. Their faces were etched with concern and relief, and the air was filled with a sense of unity and triumph.

The leaders of the coalition approached us, their expressions filled with pride and gratitude. Hilda, the village leader of Eldor, spoke first. "You have done it, Guardians. You have faced the darkness and emerged victorious. We are forever in your debt."

Clara, ever the voice of reason, replied, "This victory belongs to all of us. Our unity and strength have guided us through the darkest of times."

Lucas added, "The power of the Guardians has been our greatest ally, but we must remember that the light within us is what truly matters."

Elara nodded in agreement. "We have shown that when we stand together, we can overcome any challenge."

Alaric, his presence radiating confidence, said, "Our journey is not over. We must continue to protect our world and ensure that the light prevails."

As we celebrated our victory and the unity that had brought us together, I couldn't help but feel a profound sense of responsibility. The power of the Guardians had been both a blessing and a burden, and I knew that our journey was far from complete.

THAT NIGHT, AS THE moon rose high in the sky, casting its gentle light over the camp, I found a moment of quiet reflection. The weight of the sacrifices we had made hung heavy in the air, but the sense of accomplishment and hope was palpable.

I stood at the edge of the camp, gazing up at the stars. The energy of the Guardians pulsed within me, a constant reminder of the power we had harnessed and the price we had paid. The world was safe, but the journey to protect it was far from over.

Daniel joined me, his presence a comforting balm to my weary soul. "Olivia, you were incredible. Your strength and determination have inspired us all."

I smiled, feeling a deep sense of gratitude. "Thank you, Daniel. I couldn't have done it without all of you. Our unity and bond have been our greatest strength."

He took my hand, his touch warm and reassuring. "We'll face whatever comes next together, Olivia. Our bond is unbreakable, and we can handle anything."

As we stood together, the gentle light of the moon casting a soothing glow over the camp, I made a silent vow. We would continue to protect our world, no matter the cost. With the strength and resilience of our community, and the deepening bond between us, we would face whatever challenges lay ahead and build a future filled with promise and possibility.

### **CHAPTER 9: A NEW Dawn**

The Shadow Lord had been defeated, but the journey to rebuild our world was only beginning. The battle had taken its toll on all of us, and the scars of war were evident in the weary faces and wounded hearts of our friends and allies. Yet, amidst the wreckage and loss, there was a growing sense of hope and renewal. We had faced the darkness and emerged victorious, and now it was time to heal and rebuild.

As dawn broke over the camp, casting a warm golden light over the landscape, the leaders of our coalition gathered to discuss the path forward. The air was filled with a sense of determination and purpose, tempered by the recognition of the challenges that lay ahead.

Clara addressed the group, her voice steady and authoritative. "We have achieved a great victory, but our work is far from over. We must focus on rebuilding our communities and ensuring that the light we have fought for continues to shine."

Lucas nodded in agreement. "The knowledge and wisdom we have gained from the Guardians will guide us in this new era. We must use it to heal the wounds of war and strengthen our bonds."

Elara, ever the strategist, added, "We need to coordinate our efforts and work together to restore what has been lost. Our unity and determination will be our greatest assets."

Alaric, his presence radiating confidence, said, "I'll lead the efforts to secure our borders and protect our communities. We must remain vigilant and ensure that the darkness does not return."

Daniel, standing beside me, placed a reassuring hand on my shoulder. "We'll face this challenge together, Olivia. Our bond is strong, and we can rebuild our world."

I felt a surge of determination. "Let's do this. We'll rebuild our home and create a future filled with promise and possibility."

IN THE DAYS THAT FOLLOWED, we worked tirelessly to restore our communities and heal the wounds of war. The sense of unity and purpose that had guided us through the battle now fueled our efforts to rebuild. The leaders of our coalition coordinated their efforts, ensuring that resources and support were distributed to those in need.

We rebuilt homes and structures, cleared debris, and tended to the wounded. The sense of camaraderie and mutual support was palpable, and I could see the strength and resilience of our people shining through. Each act of kindness and cooperation brought us closer together, reinforcing the bonds we had forged in the heat of battle.

As we worked, I often found myself reflecting on the journey that had brought us to this point. The trials we had faced, the sacrifices we had made, and the victories we had achieved had all shaped us into a stronger, more united community. The power of the Guardians had been our greatest ally, but it was our unity and determination that had ultimately carried us through.

One evening, as the sun set and cast a warm golden light over the village, I found a moment of quiet reflection. Daniel joined me, his presence a comforting balm to my weary soul.

"Olivia," he began, his voice filled with affection, "we've come so far together. We've faced unimaginable challenges and emerged stronger. I am so proud of everything we've accomplished."

I smiled, feeling a deep sense of gratitude. "Thank you, Daniel. Our bond has been our greatest strength. Together, we can face anything."

He took my hand, his touch warm and reassuring. "We'll continue to build a future filled with hope and promise. Our journey is far from over, but I know that we can handle whatever comes next."

AS THE WEEKS TURNED into months, the village of Ravenswood and the surrounding communities flourished. The sense of unity and resilience that had guided us through the darkest of times now fueled our efforts to create a brighter future. The alliances we had forged in battle remained strong, and together, we worked to ensure that the light of the Guardians continued to shine.

The ancient texts and artifacts we had collected provided invaluable knowledge and wisdom, guiding our efforts to restore and protect our world. We established schools and training centers, passing on the teachings of the Guardians to the next generation. The power of the artifacts was carefully guarded, their energy used to support and strengthen our communities.

As we rebuilt, we also took steps to ensure that the darkness would never return. Alaric led the efforts to secure our borders, establishing watchtowers and patrols to guard against any potential threats. Clara and Lucas continued their research, uncovering new insights and strategies to protect our world.

Elara's strategic mind proved invaluable in coordinating our efforts, ensuring that resources were used efficiently and effectively. Her leadership helped us navigate the challenges of rebuilding, and her insights guided our path forward.

Through it all, the bond between us remained unbreakable. Daniel, Clara, Lucas, Elara, Alaric, and I stood side by side, our unity and determination guiding us through each step. The strength and resilience of our community were a testament to the power of unity and the enduring light within us.

THAT NIGHT, AS THE moon rose high in the sky, casting its gentle light over the village, I made a silent vow. We would continue to protect our world, no matter the cost. With the strength and resilience of our community, and the deepening bond between us, we would face whatever challenges lay ahead and build a future filled with promise and possibility.

The journey was far from over, but I knew that together, we could overcome anything. The light of the Guardians would continue to shine, guiding us through the darkness and illuminating the path to a brighter tomorrow.

### **EPILOGUE: A BRIGHTER Tomorrow**

The battle a### **Epilogue: A Brighter Tomorrow**

The battle against the Shadow Lord was behind us, and the world had begun to heal from the scars of war. The unity and determination that had guided us through the darkest of times now fueled our efforts to build a brighter future. The communities of Ravenswood, Blackwood, Eldor, and beyond had come together in a way that had never been seen before, and the bonds we had forged in battle remained unbreakable.

As the months passed, the signs of renewal and growth were everywhere. Homes were rebuilt, fields were replanted, and the sounds of laughter and life returned to the villages. The power of the Guardians continued to guide us, their wisdom and light a constant presence in our lives.

I stood on a hill overlooking Ravenswood, the village bathed in the golden light of the setting sun. The sight filled me with a deep sense of gratitude and hope. Our journey had been long and arduous, but we had emerged stronger and more united than ever.

Daniel joined me, his presence a comforting balm to my soul. "Olivia, look at what we've accomplished. The world is healing, and our communities are thriving. It's all because of you."

I smiled, feeling a deep sense of pride. "It's because of all of us, Daniel. Our unity and determination have brought us here. We've faced unimaginable challenges, and we've overcome them together."

He took my hand, his touch warm and reassuring. "Our journey is far from over, but I know that we can handle whatever comes next.

Together, we'll continue to build a future filled with promise and possibility."

IN THE WEEKS THAT FOLLOWED, we continued our efforts to strengthen our communities and ensure that the light of the Guardians remained a guiding force. Schools and training centers were established, passing on the teachings of the Guardians to the next generation. The power of the artifacts was carefully guarded, their energy used to support and protect our world.

Alaric led the efforts to secure our borders, establishing watchtowers and patrols to guard against any potential threats. Clara and Lucas continued their research, uncovering new insights and strategies to protect our world. Elara's strategic mind proved invaluable in coordinating our efforts, ensuring that resources were used efficiently and effectively.

The alliances we had forged in battle remained strong, and together, we worked to create a brighter future. The sense of unity and resilience that had guided us through the darkest of times now fueled our efforts to build a world filled with hope and promise.

ONE EVENING, AS THE sun set and cast a warm golden light over the village, we gathered in the town square to celebrate our achievements and reflect on the journey that had brought us here. The air was filled with a sense of joy and camaraderie, and the sounds of laughter and music echoed through the streets.

Hilda, the village leader of Eldor, stood before the gathered crowd, her voice filled with pride and gratitude. "Tonight, we celebrate our victory and the unity that has brought us here. We have faced darkness and emerged stronger. Our communities are thriving, and the light of the Guardians continues to guide us."

Clara stepped forward, her voice steady and authoritative. "Our journey is far from over, but we have shown that when we stand together, we can overcome any challenge. The future is bright, and we will continue to protect our world and build a future filled with promise and possibility."

Lucas nodded in agreement. "The knowledge and wisdom of the Guardians will continue to guide us. We must use it to heal, protect, and strengthen our communities."

Elara, ever the strategist, added, "Our unity and determination are our greatest strengths. We must continue to work together to ensure that the light within us continues to shine."

Alaric, his presence radiating confidence, said, "We have faced unimaginable challenges, and we have emerged victorious. Our journey is far from over, but I know that together, we can handle whatever comes next."

Daniel, standing beside me, placed a reassuring hand on my shoulder. "Olivia, you have been our guiding light. Your strength and determination have inspired us all. Together, we will continue to build a future filled with hope and promise."

As we stood together, the gentle light of the moon casting a soothing glow over the village, I made a silent vow. We would continue to protect our world, no matter the cost. With the strength and resilience of our community, and the deepening bond between us, we would face whatever challenges lay ahead and build a future filled with promise and possibility.

The journey was far from over, but I knew that together, we could overcome anything. The light of the Guardians would continue to shine, guiding us through the darkness and illuminating the path to a brighter tomorrow.

THIS CHAPTER SERVES as an epilogue, highlighting the rebuilding and healing efforts after the final battle and emphasizing themes of unity, resilience, and hope. The characters' commitment to creating a brighter future is showcased as they reflect on their journey and prepare for the challenges ahead. Let me know if you'd like to make any adjustments or if there's anything else I can do for you!gainst the Shadow Lord was behind us, and the world had begun to heal from the scars of war. The unity and determination that had guided us through the darkest of times now fueled our efforts to build a brighter future. The communities of Ravenswood, Blackwood, Eldor, and beyond had come together in a way that had never been seen before, and the bonds we had forged in battle remained unbreakable.

As the months passed, the signs of renewal and growth were everywhere. Homes were rebuilt, fields were replanted, and the sounds of laughter and life returned to the villages. The power of the Guardians continued to guide us, their wisdom and light a constant presence in our lives.

I stood on a hill overlooking Ravenswood, the village bathed in the golden light of the setting sun. The sight filled me with a deep sense of gratitude and hope. Our journey had been long and arduous, but we had emerged stronger and more united than ever.

Daniel joined me, his presence a comforting balm to my soul. "Olivia, look at what we've accomplished. The world is healing, and our communities are thriving. It's all because of you."

I smiled, feeling a deep sense of pride. "It's because of all of us, Daniel. Our unity and determination have brought us here. We've faced unimaginable challenges, and we've overcome them together."

He took my hand, his touch warm and reassuring. "Our journey is far from over, but I know that we can handle whatever comes next.

Together, we'll continue to build a future filled with promise and possibility."

IN THE WEEKS THAT FOLLOWED, we continued our efforts to strengthen our communities and ensure that the light of the Guardians remained a guiding force. Schools and training centers were established, passing on the teachings of the Guardians to the next generation. The power of the artifacts was carefully guarded, their energy used to support and protect our world.

Alaric led the efforts to secure our borders, establishing watchtowers and patrols to guard against any potential threats. Clara and Lucas continued their research, uncovering new insights and strategies to protect our world. Elara's strategic mind proved invaluable in coordinating our efforts, ensuring that resources were used efficiently and effectively.

The alliances we had forged in battle remained strong, and together, we worked to create a brighter future. The sense of unity and resilience that had guided us through the darkest of times now fueled our efforts to build a world filled with hope and promise.

ONE EVENING, AS THE sun set and cast a warm golden light over the village, we gathered in the town square to celebrate our achievements and reflect on the journey that had brought us here. The air was filled with a sense of joy and camaraderie, and the sounds of laughter and music echoed through the streets.

Hilda, the village leader of Eldor, stood before the gathered crowd, her voice filled with pride and gratitude. "Tonight, we celebrate our victory and the unity that has brought us here. We have faced darkness and emerged stronger. Our communities are thriving, and the light of the Guardians continues to guide us."

Clara stepped forward, her voice steady and authoritative. "Our journey is far from over, but we have shown that when we stand together, we can overcome any challenge. The future is bright, and we will continue to protect our world and build a future filled with promise and possibility."

Lucas nodded in agreement. "The knowledge and wisdom of the Guardians will continue to guide us. We must use it to heal, protect, and strengthen our communities."

Elara, ever the strategist, added, "Our unity and determination are our greatest strengths. We must continue to work together to ensure that the light within us continues to shine."

Alaric, his presence radiating confidence, said, "We have faced unimaginable challenges, and we have emerged victorious. Our journey is far from over, but I know that together, we can handle whatever comes next."

Daniel, standing beside me, placed a reassuring hand on my shoulder. "Olivia, you have been our guiding light. Your strength and determination have inspired us all. Together, we will continue to build a future filled with hope and promise."

As we stood together, the gentle light of the moon casting a soothing glow over the village, I made a silent vow. We would continue to protect our world, no matter the cost. With the strength and resilience of our community, and the deepening bond between us, we would face whatever challenges lay ahead and build a future filled with promise and possibility.

The journey was far from over, but I knew that together, we could overcome anything. The light of the Guardians would continue to shine, guiding us through the darkness and illuminating the path to a brighter tomorrow.

### **CHAPTER 10: THE Legacy of the Guardians**

Months turned into years, and the world continued to thrive under the guidance of the Guardians' wisdom and the unity of our communities. The dark days of the Shadow Lord's reign became a distant memory, and the light of the Guardians shone brightly, illuminating our path forward. The lessons we had learned and the bonds we had forged continued to shape our journey, and our commitment to protecting our world remained unwavering.

As the seasons changed, we saw the fruits of our labor in the flourishing fields, the bustling markets, and the laughter of children playing in the streets. The sense of hope and renewal was palpable, and it filled our hearts with gratitude and determination.

One crisp autumn morning, as the leaves painted the landscape in vibrant hues of red and gold, I stood at the edge of the forest, reflecting on the journey that had brought us here. The air was cool, and the scent of pine and earth filled my senses. I felt a profound connection to the land and the people who had fought to protect it.

Daniel joined me, his presence a comforting balm to my soul. "Olivia, look at what we've accomplished. Our world is thriving, and our communities are stronger than ever."

I smiled, feeling a deep sense of pride and gratitude. "It's because of all of us, Daniel. Our unity and determination have brought us here. We've faced unimaginable challenges, and we've overcome them together."

He took my hand, his touch warm and reassuring. "Our journey is far from over, but I know that we can handle whatever comes next. Together, we'll continue to build a future filled with promise and possibility."

IN THE YEARS THAT FOLLOWED, we continued to build on the foundations we had laid. Schools and training centers flourished, passing on the teachings of the Guardians to the next generation. The power of the artifacts was carefully guarded, their energy used to support and protect our world.

Alaric's efforts to secure our borders and protect our communities proved invaluable. Watchtowers and patrols ensured that any potential threats were swiftly dealt with, and the sense of safety and security allowed our communities to thrive.

Clara and Lucas's research continued to uncover new insights and strategies to protect our world. Their dedication to understanding the power of the Guardians and the balance between light and darkness guided our efforts to create a harmonious and just society.

Elara's strategic mind remained a guiding force in our efforts to rebuild and strengthen our communities. Her leadership and vision helped us navigate the challenges of growth and change, ensuring that our resources were used efficiently and effectively.

Through it all, the bond between us remained unbreakable. Daniel, Clara, Lucas, Elara, Alaric, and I stood side by side, our unity and determination guiding us through each step. The strength and resilience of our community were a testament to the power of unity and the enduring light within us.

ONE EVENING, AS THE sun set and cast a warm golden light over the village, we gathered in the town square to celebrate the annual Festival of Light. The air was filled with the sounds of laughter and music, and the scent of delicious food wafted through the streets. The festival was a time to reflect on our journey, celebrate our achievements, and look forward to the future.

As I stood on the stage, addressing the gathered crowd, I felt a deep sense of pride and gratitude. "Tonight, we celebrate the light within us and the unity that has brought us here. We have faced darkness and emerged stronger. Our communities are thriving, and the legacy of the Guardians continues to guide us."

The crowd erupted in cheers, their faces filled with joy and hope. The sense of camaraderie and mutual support was palpable, and I could see the strength and resilience of our people shining through.

Daniel, Clara, Lucas, Elara, and Alaric joined me on the stage, their presence a testament to the bonds we had forged and the journey we had undertaken. Together, we looked out at the faces of our friends and allies, our hearts filled with hope and determination.

AS THE FESTIVAL CONTINUED, I found a moment of quiet reflection, standing at the edge of the village and gazing up at the stars. The night was clear, and the constellations seemed to twinkle with a gentle, comforting light. I felt the presence of the Guardians, their wisdom and strength a constant guide.

Daniel joined me, his presence a comforting balm to my soul. "Olivia, you have been our guiding light. Your strength and determination have inspired us all. Together, we will continue to build a future filled with hope and promise."

I smiled, feeling a deep sense of pride and gratitude. "Thank you, Daniel. Our bond has been our greatest strength. Together, we can face anything."

He took my hand, his touch warm and reassuring. "Our journey is far from over, but I know that we can handle whatever comes next. The light of the Guardians will continue to guide us, illuminating the path to a brighter tomorrow."

As we stood together, the gentle light of the stars casting a soothing glow over the village, I made a silent vow. We would continue to protect our world, no matter the cost. With the strength and resilience of our community, and the deepening bond between us, we would face

whatever challenges lay ahead and build a future filled with promise and possibility.

The legacy of the Guardians would continue to shine, guiding us through the darkness and illuminating the path to a brighter tomorrow. And together, we would build a world filled with hope, unity, and endless possibilities.

### **CHAPTER 11: NEW Horizons**

Years had passed since the final battle against the Shadow Lord, and the world we had fought to protect was thriving. The unity and determination that had guided us through the darkest times now fueled our journey towards a brighter future. The lessons we had learned, the bonds we had forged, and the legacy of the Guardians continued to shape our path.

The seasons changed, bringing new challenges and opportunities. Our communities grew stronger, and the sense of hope and renewal was palpable. We had built a world filled with promise and possibility, and the light of the Guardians shone brightly, guiding us forward.

One crisp spring morning, as the first light of dawn broke over the horizon, I stood on a hill overlooking Ravenswood. The village was bathed in the soft, golden light of the rising sun, and the sight filled me with a deep sense of gratitude and hope. The journey that had brought us here had been long and arduous, but we had emerged stronger and more united than ever.

Daniel joined me, his presence a comforting balm to my soul. "Olivia, look at what we've accomplished. Our world is thriving, and our communities are stronger than ever."

I smiled, feeling a deep sense of pride and gratitude. "It's because of all of us, Daniel. Our unity and determination have brought us here. We've faced unimaginable challenges, and we've overcome them together."

He took my hand, his touch warm and reassuring. "Our journey is far from over, but I know that we can handle whatever comes next. Together, we'll continue to build a future filled with promise and possibility."

IN THE YEARS THAT FOLLOWED, we continued to build on the foundations we had laid. Schools and training centers flourished, passing on the teachings of the Guardians to the next generation. The power of the artifacts was carefully guarded, their energy used to support and protect our world.

Alaric's efforts to secure our borders and protect our communities proved invaluable. Watchtowers and patrols ensured that any potential threats were swiftly dealt with, and the sense of safety and security allowed our communities to thrive.

Clara and Lucas's research continued to uncover new insights and strategies to protect our world. Their dedication to understanding the power of the Guardians and the balance between light and darkness guided our efforts to create a harmonious and just society.

Elara's strategic mind remained a guiding force in our efforts to rebuild and strengthen our communities. Her leadership and vision helped us navigate the challenges of growth and change, ensuring that our resources were used efficiently and effectively.

Through it all, the bond between us remained unbreakable. Daniel, Clara, Lucas, Elara, Alaric, and I stood side by side, our unity and determination guiding us through each step. The strength and resilience of our community were a testament to the power of unity and the enduring light within us.

ONE EVENING, AS THE sun set and cast a warm golden light over the village, we gathered in the town square to celebrate the annual Festival of Light. The air was filled with the sounds of laughter and music, and the scent of delicious food wafted through the streets. The festival was a time to reflect on our journey, celebrate our achievements, and look forward to the future.

As I stood on the stage, addressing the gathered crowd, I felt a deep sense of pride and gratitude. "Tonight, we celebrate the light within us and the unity that has brought us here. We have faced darkness and emerged stronger. Our communities are thriving, and the legacy of the Guardians continues to guide us."

The crowd erupted in cheers, their faces filled with joy and hope. The sense of camaraderie and mutual support was palpable, and I could see the strength and resilience of our people shining through.

Daniel, Clara, Lucas, Elara, and Alaric joined me on the stage, their presence a testament to the bonds we had forged and the journey we had undertaken. Together, we looked out at the faces of our friends and allies, our hearts filled with hope and determination.

AS THE FESTIVAL CONTINUED, I found a moment of quiet reflection, standing at the edge of the village and gazing up at the stars. The night was clear, and the constellations seemed to twinkle with a gentle, comforting light. I felt the presence of the Guardians, their wisdom and strength a constant guide.

Daniel joined me, his presence a comforting balm to my soul. "Olivia, you have been our guiding light. Your strength and determination have inspired us all. Together, we will continue to build a future filled with hope and promise."

I smiled, feeling a deep sense of pride and gratitude. "Thank you, Daniel. Our bond has been our greatest strength. Together, we can face anything."

He took my hand, his touch warm and reassuring. "Our journey is far from over, but I know that we can handle whatever comes next. The light of the Guardians will continue to guide us, illuminating the path to a brighter tomorrow."

As we stood together, the gentle light of the stars casting a soothing glow over the village, I made a silent vow. We would continue to protect our world, no matter the cost. With the strength and resilience of our community, and the deepening bond between us, we would face whatever challenges lay ahead and build a future filled with promise and possibility.

The legacy of the Guardians would continue to shine, guiding us through the darkness and illuminating the path to a brighter tomorrow. And together, we would build a world filled with hope, unity, and endless possibilities.

### **CHAPTER 12: A PROMISE of Forever**

The passage of time had not dulled the sense of wonder and gratitude that filled our hearts. Ravenswood and the surrounding communities continued to thrive, their bonds of unity and resilience growing ever stronger. The legacy of the Guardians guided us, and the light within us illuminated our path forward. It was a time of renewal and hope, and the future seemed brighter than ever.

One balmy summer evening, as the sun dipped below the horizon and painted the sky with hues of pink and orange, Daniel invited me to take a walk with him. The air was warm and filled with the sweet scent of blooming flowers, and a gentle breeze rustled the leaves in the trees. There was a serene beauty to the evening, and I could feel a sense of anticipation in the air.

We walked hand in hand through the fields, the golden light of the setting sun casting a warm glow over the landscape. Daniel's presence was a comforting balm to my soul, and I cherished these moments of quiet reflection with him.

"Olivia," Daniel began, his voice soft and filled with affection, "look at how far we've come. Our world is thriving, and our communities are stronger than ever. It's because of you."

I smiled, feeling a deep sense of pride and gratitude. "It's because of all of us, Daniel. Our unity and determination have brought us here. We've faced unimaginable challenges, and we've overcome them together."

He nodded, his eyes filled with warmth and love. "There's something I've been wanting to ask you for a long time, Olivia. Something that has been in my heart since the day we met."

My heart began to race as I sensed the gravity of his words. "What is it, Daniel?"

He stopped walking and turned to face me, taking both of my hands in his. The golden light of the sunset bathed us in its warm glow, and in that moment, the world seemed to stand still.

"Olivia," Daniel said, his voice steady and filled with emotion, "you are my guiding light. Your strength, determination, and compassion have inspired me every day. I cannot imagine my life without you by my side. I want to spend the rest of my life with you, facing every challenge and celebrating every triumph together."

He reached into his pocket and pulled out a small, ornate box. Opening it, he revealed a beautiful ring, its design simple yet elegant, with a single, radiant gemstone that seemed to capture the light of the sunset.

"Olivia," he continued, his eyes locked onto mine, "will you marry me?"

Tears welled up in my eyes as the weight of his words sank in. My heart swelled with love and joy, and I felt a sense of peace and certainty that I had never known before.

"Yes, Daniel," I whispered, my voice trembling with emotion. "Yes, I will marry you."

A radiant smile spread across his face as he slipped the ring onto my finger. The gemstone sparkled in the fading light, a symbol of our love and the promise of a future filled with hope and possibility.

We embraced, the warmth of his arms a comforting shelter from the world. In that moment, I knew that we were destined to face whatever challenges lay ahead together, our bond unbreakable and our love unwavering.

AS WE MADE OUR WAY back to the village, hand in hand, the sense of joy and excitement was palpable. We shared our news with our friends and allies, their faces lighting up with happiness and celebration. The village erupted in cheers and congratulations, and the air was filled with the sounds of laughter and music.

Clara, ever the voice of reason, was the first to embrace us. "I'm so happy for both of you. Your love has been a guiding light for all of us, and I know that together, you can face anything."

Lucas nodded in agreement, his eyes filled with warmth. "Your bond is a testament to the strength of unity and love. Congratulations, my friends."

Elara, ever the strategist, added, "This is a time of celebration and hope. Your love is a beacon of light that will guide us all."

Alaric, his presence radiating confidence, said, "You have faced unimaginable challenges and emerged stronger. Your love is a testament to the strength of your spirits. Congratulations."

THAT NIGHT, AS THE moon rose high in the sky, casting its gentle light over the village, Daniel and I found a moment of quiet reflection.

We stood at the edge of the village, gazing up at the stars, the night clear and filled with the gentle twinkle of constellations.

"Olivia," Daniel said, his voice soft and filled with love, "our journey is far from over, but I know that together, we can handle whatever comes next. The light of the Guardians will continue to guide us, illuminating the path to a brighter tomorrow."

I smiled, feeling a deep sense of pride and gratitude. "Thank you, Daniel. Our bond has been our greatest strength. Together, we can face anything."

He took my hand, his touch warm and reassuring. "We'll continue to build a future filled with hope and promise. Our love will guide us through whatever challenges lie ahead."

As we stood together, the gentle light of the stars casting a soothing glow over the village, I made a silent vow. We would continue to protect our world, no matter the cost. With the strength and resilience of our community, and the deepening bond between us, we would face whatever challenges lay ahead and build a future filled with promise and possibility.

The legacy of the Guardians would continue to shine, guiding us through the darkness and illuminating the path to a brighter tomorrow. And together, we would build a world filled with hope, unity, and endless possibilities.

### **CHAPTER 13: A NEW Beginning**

In the days following Daniel's proposal, the village of Ravenswood was filled with a renewed sense of joy and excitement. The news of our engagement spread quickly, and the entire community came together to celebrate. The warmth and support from our friends and neighbors were overwhelming, and I felt a deep sense of gratitude for the bonds we had forged and the journey we had undertaken together.

One sunny morning, Clara, Elara, and I gathered in the village square to begin planning the wedding. The air was filled with the sweet scent of blooming flowers, and the sounds of laughter and conversation echoed through the streets. It was a time of renewal and hope, and I couldn't help but feel a sense of anticipation for the future.

"Olivia, your wedding is going to be beautiful," Clara said, her voice filled with excitement. "The whole village is coming together to help. It's going to be a celebration of love and unity."

Elara, ever the strategist, added, "We'll make sure everything is perfect. The decorations, the food, the music—everything will reflect the joy and love that you and Daniel share."

I smiled, feeling a deep sense of gratitude. "Thank you both. Your support means the world to me. I couldn't have asked for better friends."

As we discussed the details of the wedding, I felt a sense of joy and contentment that I had never known before. The journey that had brought us here had been filled with challenges and sacrifices, but it had also brought us closer together and strengthened our bonds.

THE DAYS LEADING UP to the wedding were filled with excitement and activity. The village was transformed into a vibrant tapestry of colors, with flowers and decorations adorning every corner. The sounds of music and laughter filled the air, and the sense of unity and celebration was palpable.

Daniel and I spent our days preparing for the wedding, surrounded by the love and support of our friends and family. The anticipation and joy were contagious, and I couldn't help but feel a sense of wonder at the beauty and magic of it all.

One evening, as the sun set and cast a warm golden light over the village, Daniel and I found a moment of quiet reflection. We stood at the edge of the village, gazing up at the stars, the night clear and filled with the gentle twinkle of constellations.

"Olivia," Daniel said, his voice soft and filled with love, "our journey is far from over, but I know that together, we can handle whatever comes next. The light of the Guardians will continue to guide us, illuminating the path to a brighter tomorrow."

I smiled, feeling a deep sense of pride and gratitude. "Thank you, Daniel. Our bond has been our greatest strength. Together, we can face anything."

He took my hand, his touch warm and reassuring. "We'll continue to build a future filled with hope and promise. Our love will guide us through whatever challenges lie ahead."

As we stood together, the gentle light of the stars casting a soothing glow over the village, I made a silent vow. We would continue to protect our world, no matter the cost. With the strength and resilience of our community, and the deepening bond between us, we would face whatever challenges lay ahead and build a future filled with promise and possibility.

THE DAY OF THE WEDDING arrived, and the village of Ravenswood was a sight to behold. The sun shone brightly, casting a warm, golden light over the landscape. The air was filled with the sweet scent of blooming flowers, and the sounds of music and laughter echoed through the streets.

As I prepared for the ceremony, surrounded by Clara, Elara, and my closest friends, I felt a sense of calm and contentment wash over me. The love and support of my community were a constant source of strength, and I knew that I was about to embark on a new journey filled with hope and promise.

Clara smiled warmly as she helped me with the final touches of my dress. "Olivia, you look absolutely stunning. This is your day, and it's going to be perfect."

Elara nodded in agreement. "Everything is ready. The decorations, the food, the music—everything reflects the joy and love that you and Daniel share. This is a celebration of your love and the unity of our community."

I took a deep breath, feeling a surge of excitement and anticipation. "Thank you both. Your support means the world to me. I couldn't have asked for better friends."

THE CEREMONY TOOK PLACE in the village square, surrounded by the beauty of nature and the love of our friends and family. The air was filled with the sounds of music and laughter, and the sense of unity and celebration was palpable.

As I walked down the aisle, my heart swelled with love and joy. Daniel stood at the altar, his eyes filled with warmth and affection. The sight of him waiting for me filled me with a sense of peace and certainty, and I knew that we were meant to be together.

The ceremony was a beautiful reflection of our journey and the bonds we had forged. Clara and Lucas spoke words of love and unity, while Elara and Alaric offered their blessings and support. The sense of joy and celebration was overwhelming, and I couldn't help but feel a deep sense of gratitude for the love and support of our community.

When it was time for our vows, Daniel took my hands in his, his touch warm and reassuring. "Olivia, you are my guiding light. Your strength, determination, and compassion have inspired me every day. I promise to stand by your side, to love and support you, and to face every challenge together."

Tears welled up in my eyes as I spoke my vows. "Daniel, you are my rock, my partner, and my best friend. Your love and support have been a constant source of strength. I promise to stand by your side, to love and support you, and to face every challenge together."

As we exchanged rings and sealed our vows with a kiss, the village erupted in cheers and applause. The sense of unity and celebration was palpable, and I felt a deep sense of joy and contentment.

THAT NIGHT, AS THE moon rose high in the sky, casting its gentle light over the village, Daniel and I found a moment of quiet reflection. We stood at the edge of the village, gazing up at the stars, the night clear and filled with the gentle twinkle of constellations.

"Olivia," Daniel said, his voice soft and filled with love, "today has been the most beautiful day of my life. Our journey is far from over, but I know that together, we can handle whatever comes next. The light of the Guardians will continue to guide us, illuminating the path to a brighter tomorrow."

I smiled, feeling a deep sense of pride and gratitude. "Thank you, Daniel. Our bond has been our greatest strength. Together, we can face anything."

He took my hand, his touch warm and reassuring. "We'll continue to build a future filled with hope and promise. Our love will guide us through whatever challenges lie ahead."

As we stood together, the gentle light of the stars casting a soothing glow over the village, I made a silent vow. We would continue to protect our world, no matter the cost. With the strength and resilience of our community, and the deepening bond between us, we would face whatever challenges lay ahead and build a future filled with promise and possibility.

The legacy of the Guardians would continue to shine, guiding us through the darkness and illuminating the path to a brighter tomorrow. And together, we would build a world filled with hope, unity, and endless possibilities.

### **CHAPTER 14: THE Whisper of Shadows**

The joy and celebration of our wedding carried us through many months of peace and prosperity. Ravenswood and the surrounding communities continued to flourish, their bonds of unity and resilience growing ever stronger. The light of the Guardians guided us, and the legacy we had built filled our hearts with hope and determination.

One crisp autumn evening, as the leaves turned vibrant shades of red and gold, Daniel and I were enjoying a quiet moment together. We stood at the edge of the forest, the air filled with the scent of pine and earth. The tranquility of the moment was a stark contrast to the challenges we had faced, and I felt a deep sense of contentment.

As we gazed out over the landscape, a sudden chill ran down my spine. The air seemed to grow colder, and a sense of unease settled over me. I glanced at Daniel, whose expression mirrored my own feelings of apprehension.

"Do you feel that?" I asked, my voice barely above a whisper. "Something isn't right."

Daniel nodded, his eyes scanning the horizon. "I feel it too, Olivia. It's as if a shadow has fallen over the land."

Just then, a figure emerged from the shadows of the forest. Cloaked in darkness, their presence exuded an aura of malevolence and power. The figure's eyes gleamed with an unnatural light, and a sinister smile played on their lips.

"Greetings, Guardians," the figure said, their voice a chilling whisper that seemed to echo through the trees. "I have been watching you."

I stepped forward, my heart pounding with a mixture of fear and determination. "Who are you? What do you want?"

The figure chuckled softly, their laughter sending shivers down my spine. "I am known as the Whisper of Shadows, and I have come to reclaim what is rightfully mine. The light of the Guardians may have prevailed before, but the darkness is eternal. You cannot escape it."

Daniel moved to stand beside me, his presence a source of strength and support. "We will not let you harm our world. The unity and strength of our community will protect us."

The Whisper of Shadows' eyes gleamed with a malevolent light. "We shall see, Guardians. The shadows are always watching, waiting for the right moment to strike. And when they do, you will understand the true power of the darkness."

With that, the figure vanished into the shadows, leaving us with a sense of foreboding and uncertainty. The encounter had shaken us to our core, and I knew that a new threat had emerged.

AS NEWS OF THE WHISPER of Shadows spread throughout the village, the sense of unease grew stronger. Our friends and allies gathered to discuss the threat and formulate a plan. The atmosphere was tense, and the weight of the situation hung heavy in the air.

Clara addressed the group, her voice steady but filled with concern. "We cannot underestimate this new threat. The Whisper of Shadows is unlike anything we've faced before. We must be prepared for anything."

Lucas nodded in agreement. "The darkness they wield is powerful, but so is the light within us. We must rely on our unity and the wisdom of the Guardians to guide us through this challenge."

Elara, ever the strategist, added, "We need to strengthen our defenses and remain vigilant. The Whisper of Shadows could strike at any moment, and we must be ready."

Alaric, his presence radiating confidence, said, "I'll lead the efforts to secure our borders and protect our communities. We cannot let the darkness take hold."

Daniel, standing beside me, placed a reassuring hand on my shoulder. "We'll face this together, Olivia. Our bond is strong, and we can handle anything."

I took a deep breath, feeling the weight of the responsibility before us. "Let's do this. We'll protect our home and stand against the Whisper of Shadows."

IN THE DAYS THAT FOLLOWED, we worked tirelessly to prepare for the impending threat. The sense of unity and determination that had guided us through past challenges now fueled our efforts to protect our world from the Whisper of Shadows. We fortified our defenses, trained our warriors, and strengthened our bonds.

The power of the Guardians continued to guide us, their wisdom and light a constant presence. We studied ancient texts and artifacts, seeking any knowledge that could help us understand and combat the darkness. The sense of urgency and resolve grew stronger with each passing day.

One evening, as the sun set and cast a warm golden light over the village, Daniel and I found a moment of quiet reflection. We stood at the edge of the village, gazing up at the stars, the night clear and filled with the gentle twinkle of constellations.

"Olivia," Daniel said, his voice soft and filled with determination, "we've faced unimaginable challenges before, and we've overcome them together. This new threat may be formidable, but I know that we can handle it. The light of the Guardians will continue to guide us."

I smiled, feeling a deep sense of pride and gratitude. "Thank you, Daniel. Our bond has been our greatest strength. Together, we can face anything."

He took my hand, his touch warm and reassuring. "We'll continue to build a future filled with hope and promise. Our love will guide us through whatever challenges lie ahead."

As we stood together, the gentle light of the stars casting a soothing glow over the village, I made a silent vow. We would continue to protect our world, no matter the cost. With the strength and resilience of our community, and the deepening bond between us, we would face the Whisper of Shadows and build a future filled with promise and possibility.

The legacy of the Guardians would continue to shine, guiding us through the darkness and illuminating the path to a brighter tomorrow. And together, we would stand against the new threat, our unity and determination unwavering.

WITH THE EMERGENCE of the Whisper of Shadows, our peaceful days were once again tinged with a sense of foreboding. The knowledge that a new, malevolent force was lurking in the shadows weighed heavily on all of us. Yet, our unity and determination had carried us through past challenges, and we were resolved to face this new threat with the same strength and courage.

### **Chapter 15: Shadows of Doubt**

As the days turned into weeks, the presence of the Whisper of Shadows began to cast a long shadow over our daily lives. Strange occurrences and unexplained phenomena started to plague the village. Crops withered overnight, animals disappeared without a trace, and a sense of unease settled over the community. It was clear that the Whisper of Shadows was making their presence known.

One evening, as we gathered in the council chamber to discuss the recent events, the atmosphere was tense and filled with uncertainty. Our friends and allies looked to us for guidance and reassurance, their faces etched with concern.

"We cannot ignore these signs," Clara said, her voice steady but filled with worry. "The Whisper of Shadows is testing our resolve. We must find a way to protect our village and uncover the source of this darkness."

Lucas nodded, his eyes filled with determination. "We need to understand the nature of this threat. The ancient texts may hold clues that can help us. We must study them and find a way to counter the darkness."

Elara, ever the strategist, added, "We should also increase our patrols and defenses. The Whisper of Shadows could strike at any moment, and we need to be ready."

Alaric, his presence radiating confidence, said, "I'll lead the efforts to secure our borders and protect our communities. We cannot let the darkness take hold."

Daniel, standing beside me, placed a reassuring hand on my shoulder. "We'll face this together, Olivia. Our bond is strong, and we can handle anything."

I took a deep breath, feeling the weight of the responsibility before us. "Let's do this. We'll protect our home and stand against the Whisper of Shadows."

IN THE DAYS THAT FOLLOWED, we worked tirelessly to fortify our defenses and uncover any information that could help us understand the nature of the Whisper of Shadows. The sense of unity and determination that had guided us through past challenges now fueled our efforts to protect our world from this new threat.

We studied ancient texts and artifacts, seeking any knowledge that could help us combat the darkness. Lucas's research uncovered references to a powerful artifact known as the "Mirror of Shadows," said to have the ability to reveal the true nature of any darkness it reflected.

"This mirror could be the key to understanding the Whisper of Shadows," Lucas explained, his voice filled with excitement. "If we can find it, we may be able to uncover their true intentions and weaknesses."

Elara nodded thoughtfully. "The texts mention that the mirror is hidden in the Temple of Whispers, an ancient structure located deep within the Forbidden Forest. It's a treacherous journey, but we must retrieve it if we are to stand a chance."

Alaric's eyes gleamed with determination. "I'll lead a team to the Temple of Whispers. We must retrieve the mirror and bring it back to Ravenswood."

AS WE PREPARED FOR the journey to the Temple of Whispers, the sense of anticipation and resolve grew stronger. Daniel, Alaric, Clara, Lucas, Elara, and I set out with a small group of skilled warriors and scouts, determined to retrieve the mirror and uncover the true nature of the Whisper of Shadows.

The journey through the Forbidden Forest was filled with challenges and dangers. The dense foliage and treacherous terrain tested our endurance and resolve. We encountered dark creatures and twisted beings, their malevolent presence a constant reminder of the darkness we faced. Yet, our unity and determination guided us through each obstacle.

After days of navigating the forest, we finally reached the Temple of Whispers. The ancient structure was shrouded in darkness, its walls covered in intricate carvings and symbols. The air was thick with an oppressive energy, and I could feel the weight of the darkness pressing down on us.

"This is it," Lucas said, his voice filled with reverence. "The Mirror of Shadows is inside. We must proceed with caution."

Alaric led the way, his combat skills and strategic mind proving invaluable. As we entered the temple, the air grew colder, and the light from our torches flickered in the darkness. The walls were lined with ancient relics and artifacts, each one holding a piece of history and knowledge.

We soon came upon a large chamber, at the center of which stood a pedestal holding the Mirror of Shadows. The mirror's surface was dark and reflective, its presence exuding an aura of power and mystery.

"This is it," Lucas said, his voice filled with awe. "The Mirror of Shadows. We must retrieve it and bring it back to Ravenswood."

As I reached out to touch the mirror, a surge of energy flowed through me, filling me with a sense of strength and clarity. The mirror's surface shimmered, revealing glimpses of hidden truths and unseen forces.

With the Mirror of Shadows in our possession, we began the journey back to Ravenswood. The sense of accomplishment and hope was palpable, and I knew that we were one step closer to uncovering the true nature of the Whisper of Shadows.

THAT NIGHT, AS THE moon rose high in the sky, casting its gentle light over the camp, Daniel and I found a moment of quiet reflection. We stood at the edge of the camp, gazing up at the stars, the night clear and filled with the gentle twinkle of constellations.

"Olivia," Daniel said, his voice soft and filled with determination, "we've faced unimaginable challenges before, and we've overcome them together. This new threat may be formidable, but I know that we can handle it. The light of the Guardians will continue to guide us."

I smiled, feeling a deep sense of pride and gratitude. "Thank you, Daniel. Our bond has been our greatest strength. Together, we can face anything."

He took my hand, his touch warm and reassuring. "We'll continue to build a future filled with hope and promise. Our love will guide us through whatever challenges lie ahead."

As we stood together, the gentle light of the stars casting a soothing glow over the camp, I made a silent vow. We would continue to protect our world, no matter the cost. With the strength and resilience of our community, and the deepening bond between us, we would face the Whisper of Shadows and build a future filled with promise and possibility.

The legacy of the Guardians would continue to shine, guiding us through the darkness and illuminating the path to a brighter tomorrow. And together, we would stand against the new threat, our unity and determination unwavering.

### **CHAPTER 17: SHADOWS of Conflict**

The revelation of the Whisper of Shadows through the Mirror of Shadows brought a new sense of urgency and resolve to our efforts. We knew that the darkness would return, and we had to be prepared for the impending conflict. The unity and determination that had guided us through past challenges now fueled our resolve to protect our world from this new threat.

In the days that followed, we worked tirelessly to strengthen our defenses and uncover any information that could help us understand the Whisper of Shadows' intentions and weaknesses. The sense of unity and determination was palpable, and our community came together to face the challenge ahead.

One evening, as the sun set and cast a warm golden light over the village, we gathered in the council chamber to discuss our strategy. The atmosphere was tense, but the resolve in the room was unwavering.

Clara addressed the group, her voice steady and authoritative. "We have uncovered the true nature of the Whisper of Shadows, but our work is far from over. We must be prepared for their return and ensure that our defenses are impenetrable."

Lucas nodded, his eyes filled with determination. "The Mirror of Shadows has revealed important clues about their intentions. We must use this knowledge to strengthen our strategy and protect our world."

Elara, ever the strategist, added, "We need to coordinate our efforts and ensure that our resources are used efficiently and effectively. The Whisper of Shadows will not stop until they have achieved their goal."

Alaric, his presence radiating confidence, said, "I'll lead the efforts to secure our borders and protect our communities. We cannot let the darkness take hold."

Daniel, standing beside me, placed a reassuring hand on my shoulder. "We'll face this together, Olivia. Our bond is strong, and we can handle anything."

I took a deep breath, feeling the weight of the responsibility before us. "Let's do this. We'll protect our home and stand against the Whisper of Shadows."

IN THE WEEKS THAT FOLLOWED, our efforts to strengthen our defenses and prepare for the impending conflict intensified. The sense of unity and determination that had guided us through past challenges now fueled our resolve to protect our world from the Whisper of Shadows.

We fortified our borders, trained our warriors, and enhanced our magical defenses. The power of the Guardians continued to guide us, their wisdom and light a constant presence. We studied the ancient texts and artifacts, seeking any knowledge that could help us understand and combat the darkness.

One evening, as the sun set and cast a warm golden light over the village, Daniel and I found a moment of quiet reflection. We stood at the edge of the village, gazing up at the stars, the night clear and filled with the gentle twinkle of constellations.

"Olivia," Daniel said, his voice soft and filled with determination, "we've faced unimaginable challenges before, and we've overcome them together. This new threat may be formidable, but I know that we can handle it. The light of the Guardians will continue to guide us."

I smiled, feeling a deep sense of pride and gratitude. "Thank you, Daniel. Our bond has been our greatest strength. Together, we can face anything."

He took my hand, his touch warm and reassuring. "We'll continue to build a future filled with hope and promise. Our love will guide us through whatever challenges lie ahead."

AS THE WEEKS TURNED into months, the sense of anticipation and resolve grew stronger. We knew that the Whisper of Shadows would return, and we had to be ready. Our preparations were thorough, and our unity was unwavering.

One crisp autumn morning, as the first light of dawn broke over the horizon, a scout arrived with urgent news. The Whisper of Shadows had been spotted on the outskirts of our territory, their dark presence a chilling reminder of the threat we faced.

The council chamber was filled with tension as we gathered to discuss the news. Our friends and allies looked to us for guidance, their faces etched with concern.

"We knew this day would come," Clara said, her voice steady and resolute. "The Whisper of Shadows is making their move. We must be prepared to defend our world."

Lucas nodded, his eyes filled with determination. "The Mirror of Shadows has revealed important information about their weaknesses. We must use this knowledge to our advantage."

Elara, ever the strategist, added, "We need to coordinate our efforts and ensure that our defenses are impenetrable. The Whisper of Shadows will not stop until they have achieved their goal."

Alaric, his presence radiating confidence, said, "I'll lead the charge. Our warriors are ready, and our defenses are strong. We will not let the darkness take hold."

Daniel, standing beside me, placed a reassuring hand on my shoulder. "We'll face this together, Olivia. Our bond is strong, and we can handle anything."

I took a deep breath, feeling the weight of the responsibility before us. "Let's do this. We'll protect our home and stand against the Whisper of Shadows."

AS THE SUN SET AND cast a warm golden light over the village, our forces prepared for the impending battle. The sense of unity and determination was palpable, and our resolve to protect our world was unwavering.

The Whisper of Shadows' forces approached, their dark presence a stark contrast to the radiant light of our defenses. The air was thick with tension as we faced our enemies, our hearts pounding with a mixture of fear and determination.

Clara, Lucas, Elara, Alaric, Daniel, and I stood at the forefront of our defenses, our unity and resolve guiding us through the impending conflict.

"Guardians," the Whisper of Shadows' voice echoed through the air, their presence exuding an aura of malevolence and power. "You cannot escape the darkness. It is eternal, and it will consume you."

I stepped forward, my heart pounding with a mixture of fear and determination. "We will not let you harm our world. The unity and strength of our community will protect us."

With a surge of energy, the battle began. The clash of light and darkness filled the air, the sounds of combat echoing through the landscape. Our forces moved with precision and unity, their determination unwavering.

As the battle raged on, I felt the power of the Guardians surging within me. Drawing upon the energy of the Mirror of Shadows, I channeled a brilliant beam of light that pierced through the darkness, striking the Whisper of Shadows' forces with precision.

The Whisper of Shadows recoiled, their form flickering and wavering. "You may have uncovered my presence, but you cannot defeat me, Guardians. The darkness will always return."

With a final, desperate effort, the shadowy figure vanished into the depths of the night, leaving us with a sense of foreboding and uncertainty. The battle was far from over, but our unity and determination had carried us through the first wave.

THAT NIGHT, AS THE moon rose high in the sky, casting its gentle light over the village, Daniel and I found a moment of quiet reflection. We stood at the edge of the village, gazing up at the stars, the night clear and filled with the gentle twinkle of constellations.

"Olivia," Daniel said, his voice soft and filled with determination, "we've faced unimaginable challenges before, and we've overcome them together. This new threat may be formidable, but I know that we can handle it. The light of the Guardians will continue to guide us."

I smiled, feeling a deep sense of pride and gratitude. "Thank you, Daniel. Our bond has been our greatest strength. Together, we can face anything."

He took my hand, his touch warm and reassuring. "We'll continue to build a future filled with hope and promise. Our love will guide us through whatever challenges lie ahead."

As we stood together, the gentle light of the stars casting a soothing glow over the village, I made a silent vow. We would continue to protect our world, no matter the cost. With the strength and resilience of our community, and the deepening bond between us, we would face the Whisper of Shadows and build a future filled with promise and possibility.

The legacy of the Guardians would continue to shine, guiding us through the darkness and illuminating the path to a brighter tomorrow. And together, we would stand against the new threat, our unity and determination unwavering.

### **CHAPTER 18: ECHOES of the Past**

The Whisper of Shadows had retreated for now, but we knew that the threat was far from over. Our unity and determination had carried us through the initial conflict, but the battle had left us with more questions than answers. The darkness was always lurking, and we needed to understand its origins to truly defeat it.

One crisp autumn morning, as the first light of dawn broke over the horizon, Lucas approached us with a sense of urgency. He carried an ancient scroll, its parchment yellowed with age and its script filled with intricate symbols.

"I've been studying the ancient texts," Lucas began, his voice filled with determination. "I believe I've found a clue about the origins of the Whisper of Shadows. There's an old legend that speaks of a powerful artifact known as the Shadowstone. It is said to be the source of their power."

Clara's eyes widened with interest. "The Shadowstone? If we can find it, we may be able to weaken the Whisper of Shadows and end their threat once and for all."

Elara, ever the strategist, added, "The legend speaks of the Shadowstone being hidden in the Ruins of Azura, an ancient city that was lost to time. It's a dangerous journey, but we must retrieve it if we are to stand a chance."

Alaric, his presence radiating confidence, said, "I'll lead a team to the Ruins of Azura. We must retrieve the Shadowstone and bring it back to Ravenswood."

Daniel, standing beside me, placed a reassuring hand on my shoulder. "We'll face this together, Olivia. Our bond is strong, and we can handle anything."

I took a deep breath, feeling the weight of the responsibility before us. "Let's do this. We'll uncover the origins of the Whisper of Shadows and protect our world."

THE JOURNEY TO THE Ruins of Azura was filled with challenges and dangers. The dense forest and treacherous terrain tested our endurance, but our unity and determination guided us through each obstacle. As we ventured deeper into the wilderness, the sense of anticipation and resolve grew stronger.

After days of navigating the rugged landscape, we finally reached the outskirts of the Ruins of Azura. The ancient city lay in ruins, its once-grand structures now reduced to crumbling stone and overgrown vegetation. The air was thick with an oppressive energy, and I could feel the weight of history pressing down on us.

"This is it," Lucas said, his voice filled with reverence. "The Shadowstone is said to be hidden within the central temple. We must proceed with caution."

Alaric led the way, his combat skills and strategic mind proving invaluable. As we entered the ruins, the air grew colder, and the light from our torches flickered in the darkness. The walls were lined with ancient carvings and symbols, each one telling a story of a long-forgotten past.

We soon came upon the central temple, its entrance guarded by intricate mechanisms and puzzles. "These puzzles must be the key to unlocking the temple," I said, my voice filled with determination. "We need to solve them to proceed."

With careful coordination, we worked together to decipher the puzzles. Each mechanism required a combination of our skills and knowledge, and I could feel the bond between us growing stronger with each successful step.

Finally, the last puzzle clicked into place, and the heavy stone door creaked open. The chamber beyond was filled with an ethereal light, and at its center stood a pedestal holding the Shadowstone. The artifact pulsed with a dark, malevolent energy, its presence exuding an aura of power and mystery.

"This is it," Lucas said, his voice filled with awe. "The Shadowstone. We must retrieve it and bring it back to Ravenswood."

As I reached out to touch the Shadowstone, a surge of energy flowed through me, filling me with a sense of strength and clarity. The artifact's power was undeniable, and I could feel its connection to the Whisper of Shadows.

With the Shadowstone in our possession, we began the journey back to Ravenswood. The sense of accomplishment and hope was palpable, and I knew that we were one step closer to understanding and defeating the Whisper of Shadows.

AS WE APPROACHED THE village, our friends and allies greeted us with relief and curiosity. The council chamber was filled with the hum of conversation as we gathered to discuss our findings and formulate a plan.

Clara addressed the group, her voice steady and authoritative. "We have retrieved the Shadowstone, but our work is far from over. We must understand its power and use it to weaken the Whisper of Shadows."

Lucas nodded, his eyes filled with determination. "The Shadowstone is the source of their power. If we can harness its energy, we may be able to defeat them once and for all."

Elara, ever the strategist, added, "We need to proceed with caution. The Shadowstone's power is immense, and we must ensure that we use it wisely."

Alaric, his presence radiating confidence, said, "I'll oversee the preparations. We cannot afford any mistakes."

Daniel, standing beside me, placed a reassuring hand on my shoulder. "We'll face this together, Olivia. Our bond is strong, and we can handle anything."

I took a deep breath, feeling the weight of the responsibility before us. "Let's do this. We'll uncover the truth and protect our home from the Whisper of Shadows."

IN THE DAYS THAT FOLLOWED, we worked tirelessly to understand the power of the Shadowstone and uncover its secrets. The sense of unity and determination that had guided us through past challenges now fueled our efforts to protect our world from the Whisper of Shadows.

As the sun set and cast a warm golden light over the village, Daniel and I found a moment of quiet reflection. We stood at the edge of the village, gazing up at the stars, the night clear and filled with the gentle twinkle of constellations.

"Olivia," Daniel said, his voice soft and filled with determination, "we've faced unimaginable challenges before, and we've overcome them together. This new threat may be formidable, but I know that we can handle it. The light of the Guardians will continue to guide us."

I smiled, feeling a deep sense of pride and gratitude. "Thank you, Daniel. Our bond has been our greatest strength. Together, we can face anything."

He took my hand, his touch warm and reassuring. "We'll continue to build a future filled with hope and promise. Our love will guide us through whatever challenges lie ahead."

As we stood together, the gentle light of the stars casting a soothing glow over the village, I made a silent vow. We would continue to protect our world, no matter the cost. With the strength and resilience of our community, and the deepening bond between us, we would face the Whisper of Shadows and build a future filled with promise and possibility.

The legacy of the Guardians would continue to shine, guiding us through the darkness and illuminating the path to a brighter tomorrow. And together, we would stand against the new threat, our unity and determination unwavering.

### **CHAPTER 19: LIGHT and Shadow**

The days following the retrieval of the Shadowstone were filled with intense study and preparation. Our unity and determination had brought us this far, and we were resolved to use the Shadowstone's power to weaken the Whisper of Shadows and protect our world. The sense of anticipation and resolve was palpable, and our community came together to face the challenge ahead.

One crisp morning, as the first light of dawn broke over the horizon, Lucas called for an urgent meeting in the council chamber. His expression was one of excitement and determination, and I knew that he had made an important discovery.

"Everyone," Lucas began, his voice filled with purpose, "I've been studying the Shadowstone, and I believe I've uncovered a way to harness its power. The ancient texts speak of a ritual that can channel the stone's energy to weaken the Whisper of Shadows."

Clara's eyes widened with interest. "If we can weaken them, we may be able to end their threat once and for all."

Elara, ever the strategist, added, "We need to proceed with caution. The ritual will require a precise combination of magic and coordination. We must ensure that we execute it perfectly."

Alaric, his presence radiating confidence, said, "I'll oversee the preparations. We cannot afford any mistakes."

Daniel, standing beside me, placed a reassuring hand on my shoulder. "We'll face this together, Olivia. Our bond is strong, and we can handle anything."

I took a deep breath, feeling the weight of the responsibility before us. "Let's do this. We'll weaken the Whisper of Shadows and protect our home."

THE DAYS THAT FOLLOWED were filled with intense preparation and coordination. The sense of unity and determination that had guided us through past challenges now fueled our efforts to harness the power of the Shadowstone. We studied the ancient texts and artifacts, seeking any knowledge that could help us understand and execute the ritual.

Finally, the day arrived when we would perform the ritual. The village square was prepared with symbols and markings, and the Shadowstone was placed at the center, its surface pulsing with a dark, malevolent energy. The air was thick with anticipation as our friends and allies gathered to witness the event.

Clara, Lucas, Elara, Alaric, Daniel, and I stood around the Shadowstone, our hearts pounding with a mixture of fear and determination. Lucas began to recite the incantations, his voice steady and filled with purpose. The markings on the ground glowed with an ethereal light, and the air seemed to vibrate with energy.

As the incantations reached their crescendo, the surface of the Shadowstone began to shimmer and shift. A dark mist swirled within its depths, and the whispers of unseen forces filled the air. The stone's power was undeniable, and I could feel its energy resonating within me.

Suddenly, the dark mist within the Shadowstone coalesced into a shadowy figure, its eyes gleaming with malevolent intent. The Whisper of Shadows had been summoned, and their presence was both terrifying and awe-inspiring.

"Guardians," the shadowy figure hissed, its voice a chilling whisper that seemed to echo through the air. "You cannot escape the darkness. It is eternal, and it will consume you."

I stepped forward, my heart pounding with a mixture of fear and determination. "We will not let you harm our world. The unity and strength of our community will protect us."

The Whisper of Shadows' eyes gleamed with a malevolent light. "You are brave, Guardians, but your light is no match for the darkness. You will fall, and your world will be consumed."

With a surge of energy, the shadowy figure unleashed a wave of dark power that surged toward us. We responded in unison, raising our hands and channeling the power of the Shadowstone. A brilliant shield of light formed around us, deflecting the dark energy and illuminating the village square with its radiance.

"We must use the Shadowstone's power to weaken the Whisper of Shadows," Lucas called out, his voice filled with determination. "Only then can we defeat them."

As the battle raged on, I felt a surge of strength and clarity. The presence of the Guardians was strong within me, guiding my actions and strengthening my resolve. Drawing upon the energy of the Shadowstone, I focused my thoughts and channeled a brilliant beam of light that pierced through the darkness, striking the shadowy figure with precision.

The Whisper of Shadows recoiled, their form flickering and wavering. "You may have uncovered my presence, but you cannot defeat me, Guardians. The darkness will always return."

With a final, desperate effort, the shadowy figure vanished into the depths of the night, leaving us with a sense of foreboding and uncertainty. The battle had weakened the Whisper of Shadows, but the fight was far from over.

AS THE SHADOWSTONE'S power waned and the village square returned to normal, the sense of urgency and resolve grew stronger. We had weakened the Whisper of Shadows, but we knew that the battle was far from over. The darkness would return, and we had to be prepared.

That night, as the moon rose high in the sky, casting its gentle light over the village, Daniel and I found a moment of quiet reflection. We stood at the edge of the village, gazing up at the stars, the night clear and filled with the gentle twinkle of constellations.

"Olivia," Daniel said, his voice soft and filled with determination, "we've faced unimaginable challenges before, and we've overcome them together. This new threat may be formidable, but I know that we can handle it. The light of the Guardians will continue to guide us."

I smiled, feeling a deep sense of pride and gratitude. "Thank you, Daniel. Our bond has been our greatest strength. Together, we can face anything."

He took my hand, his touch warm and reassuring. "We'll continue to build a future filled with hope and promise. Our love will guide us through whatever challenges lie ahead."

As we stood together, the gentle light of the stars casting a soothing glow over the village, I made a silent vow. We would continue to protect our world, no matter the cost. With the strength and resilience of our community, and the deepening bond between us, we would face the Whisper of Shadows and build a future filled with promise and possibility.

The legacy of the Guardians would continue to shine, guiding us through the darkness and illuminating the path to a brighter tomorrow. And together, we would stand against the new threat, our unity and determination unwavering.

### **CHAPTER 20: GATHERING Storms**

The ritual with the Shadowstone had weakened the Whisper of Shadows, but we knew that this was only a temporary reprieve. The darkness was persistent, and we had to stay vigilant. The unity and determination that had guided us through past challenges would be crucial in the days to come.

In the days that followed, we continued to fortify our defenses and prepare for the next confrontation. The sense of unity and resolve was palpable, and our community came together with a renewed sense of purpose. We knew that the final battle with the Whisper of Shadows was approaching, and we had to be ready.

One evening, as the sun set and cast a warm golden light over the village, Clara called for an urgent meeting in the council chamber. Her expression was one of determination, and I could sense that she had important news to share.

"Everyone," Clara began, her voice steady and authoritative, "we have received reports of increased activity from the Whisper of Shadows. They are gathering their forces for a final assault. We must be prepared for the battle ahead."

Lucas nodded, his eyes filled with resolve. "The Shadowstone has given us valuable insights into their weaknesses. We must use this knowledge to our advantage and devise a strategy to defeat them once and for all."

Elara, ever the strategist, added, "We need to coordinate our efforts and ensure that our defenses are impenetrable. The Whisper of Shadows will not stop until they have achieved their goal."

Alaric, his presence radiating confidence, said, "I'll lead the charge. Our warriors are ready, and our defenses are strong. We will not let the darkness take hold."

Daniel, standing beside me, placed a reassuring hand on my shoulder. "We'll face this together, Olivia. Our bond is strong, and we can handle anything."

I took a deep breath, feeling the weight of the responsibility before us. "Let's do this. We'll protect our home and stand against the Whisper of Shadows."

AS THE DAYS TURNED into weeks, the sense of anticipation and resolve grew stronger. We worked tirelessly to strengthen our defenses and prepare for the impending battle. The power of the Guardians continued to guide us, their wisdom and light a constant presence.

Our friends and allies came together with a renewed sense of purpose, their determination unwavering. We fortified our borders, trained our warriors, and enhanced our magical defenses. The sense of unity and camaraderie was palpable, and I could see the strength and resilience of our community shining through.

One evening, as the sun set and cast a warm golden light over the village, Daniel and I found a moment of quiet reflection. We stood at the edge of the village, gazing up at the stars, the night clear and filled with the gentle twinkle of constellations.

"Olivia," Daniel said, his voice soft and filled with determination, "we've faced unimaginable challenges before, and we've overcome them together. This new threat may be formidable, but I know that we can handle it. The light of the Guardians will continue to guide us."

I smiled, feeling a deep sense of pride and gratitude. "Thank you, Daniel. Our bond has been our greatest strength. Together, we can face anything."

He took my hand, his touch warm and reassuring. "We'll continue to build a future filled with hope and promise. Our love will guide us through whatever challenges lie ahead."

THE NIGHT BEFORE THE anticipated battle, our forces gathered in the village square for a final council. The atmosphere was tense but filled with a sense of unity and determination. The Whisper of Shadows was a formidable foe, but our resolve was unwavering.

Clara addressed the gathered crowd, her voice steady and authoritative. "Tomorrow, we face our greatest challenge. The Whisper of Shadows will launch their final assault, and we must be prepared to defend our world. Our unity and strength will guide us through the battle ahead."

Lucas nodded in agreement. "The Shadowstone has given us valuable insights into their weaknesses. We must use this knowledge to our advantage and devise a strategy to defeat them once and for all."

Elara, ever the strategist, added, "We need to coordinate our efforts and ensure that our defenses are impenetrable. The Whisper of Shadows will not stop until they have achieved their goal."

Alaric, his presence radiating confidence, said, "I'll lead the charge. Our warriors are ready, and our defenses are strong. We will not let the darkness take hold."

Daniel, standing beside me, placed a reassuring hand on my shoulder. "We'll face this together, Olivia. Our bond is strong, and we can handle anything."

I took a deep breath, feeling the weight of the responsibility before us. "Let's do this. We'll protect our home and stand against the Whisper of Shadows."

THE MORNING OF THE battle arrived, and the village was a hive of activity. Our forces prepared for the impending conflict with a sense of purpose and resolve. The air was thick with tension as we faced our enemies, our hearts pounding with a mixture of fear and determination.

The Whisper of Shadows' forces approached, their dark presence a stark contrast to the radiant light of our defenses. The sounds of combat echoed through the landscape as the battle began in earnest. Our unity and determination guided us through each clash, our resolve unwavering.

As the battle raged on, I felt the power of the Guardians surging within me. Drawing upon the energy of the Shadowstone, I channeled a brilliant beam of light that pierced through the darkness, striking the Whisper of Shadows' forces with precision.

The Whisper of Shadows recoiled, their form flickering and wavering. "You may have weakened me, Guardians, but you cannot defeat me. The darkness will always return."

With a final, desperate effort, the shadowy figure unleashed a powerful wave of dark energy that sent us sprawling. The ground trembled with the force of the attack, and the air crackled with energy. But our unity and determination carried us through the onslaught, our resolve unshaken.

AS THE SUN SET AND cast a warm golden light over the battlefield, the sounds of combat began to wane. The Whisper of Shadows' forces were retreating, their presence a fading shadow in the light of our defenses. The battle was far from over, but our unity and determination had carried us through another day.

That night, as the moon rose high in the sky, casting its gentle light over the village, Daniel and I found a moment of quiet reflection. We stood at the edge of the village, gazing up at the stars, the night clear and filled with the gentle twinkle of constellations.

"Olivia," Daniel said, his voice soft and filled with determination, "we've faced unimaginable challenges before, and we've overcome them together. This new threat may be formidable, but I know that we can handle it. The light of the Guardians will continue to guide us."

I smiled, feeling a deep sense of pride and gratitude. "Thank you, Daniel. Our bond has been our greatest strength. Together, we can face anything."

He took my hand, his touch warm and reassuring. "We'll continue to build a future filled with hope and promise. Our love will guide us through whatever challenges lie ahead."

As we stood together, the gentle light of the stars casting a soothing glow over the village, I made a silent vow. We would continue to protect our world, no matter the cost. With the strength and resilience of our community, and the deepening bond between us, we would face the Whisper of Shadows and build a future filled with promise and possibility.

The legacy of the Guardians would continue to shine, guiding us through the darkness and illuminating the path to a brighter tomorrow. And together, we would stand against the new threat, our unity and determination unwavering.

### **CHAPTER 21: A CRUCIAL Rally**

The retreat of the Whisper of Shadows was temporary; we knew they would return with greater force. As the looming final battle approached, our determination and unity would be critical. The atmosphere in the village was a mixture of urgency and resolve, and we could feel the weight of the impending conflict.

In the following days, we focused on reinforcing our defenses and fine-tuning our strategies. The guidance of the Guardians continued to be our beacon, their wisdom and light steering us forward. Our allies rallied with a renewed sense of purpose, their determination unwavering.

One evening, as the golden light of sunset bathed the village, Clara convened an urgent meeting in the council chamber. Her expression was a mixture of determination and concern, signaling important news.

"Everyone," Clara began, her voice firm and resolute, "we've received intelligence that the Whisper of Shadows is amassing their forces for a final strike. This will be their ultimate attempt to seize control. We must stand ready to defend our realm."

Lucas, his eyes gleaming with resolve, added, "The insights from the Shadowstone have revealed critical weaknesses in their ranks. We must leverage this knowledge to develop a decisive strategy to overcome them."

Elara, ever the tactician, contributed, "We need to synchronize our efforts and ensure our defenses are unbreachable. The Whisper of Shadows will not relent until they have achieved their sinister goals."

Alaric, exuding confidence, assured, "I'll lead our warriors into battle. Our forces are prepared, and our fortifications are strong. The darkness will not prevail."

Daniel, standing by my side, offered a reassuring touch. "We'll face this together, Olivia. Our bond is our strength, and we can withstand anything."

With a deep breath, I embraced the gravity of our mission. "Let's proceed. We'll shield our home and confront the Whisper of Shadows head-on."

THE DAYS STRETCHED into weeks as the village prepared for the ultimate clash. Our focus on fortifying our defenses and training our warriors intensified. The power of the Guardians remained our steadfast guide, their wisdom a constant source of strength.

Our friends and allies united with unwavering determination, their resolve echoing through the village. The preparations were exhaustive, and the bonds we had forged grew stronger with each passing day.

The morning of the final battle dawned, and the village buzzed with activity. Our forces assembled with a sense of purpose, ready to face the imminent threat. The air was thick with tension, a reminder of the gravity of the conflict ahead.

The dark forces of the Whisper of Shadows advanced, their ominous presence a stark contrast to the light emanating from our defenses. The sounds of battle reverberated through the landscape as the fight began in earnest. Our unity and resolve guided us through each clash.

Clara, Lucas, Elara, Alaric, Daniel, and I led from the frontlines, our combined strength propelling us forward.

"Guardians," the Whisper of Shadows' voice boomed, dripping with malice, "the darkness is eternal. You cannot escape it."

Stepping forward with determination, I declared, "We will not let you desecrate our world. The unity of our community will protect us."

The battle was fierce. The clash of light and darkness filled the air, the village square a battleground. Our forces moved with precision, their resolve unshaken.

Throughout the skirmish, I felt the Guardians' power coursing through me. Drawing on the Shadowstone's energy, I unleashed a radiant beam of light, targeting the Whisper of Shadows' minions with precision.

The shadowy figures recoiled, their forms wavering. "You may have weakened us, Guardians, but you will never defeat us. The darkness will return."

With a final, desperate attack, the Whisper of Shadows unleashed a wave of dark energy, throwing us off balance. The ground quaked, the air crackled with tension. Yet, our unity endured, our resolve unwavering.

AS THE SUN SET, CASTING a warm glow over the battlefield, the sounds of combat receded. The Whisper of Shadows' forces retreated, their presence fading in the light of our defenses. The battle was far from over, but our unity had carried us through another day.

That night, under the gentle light of the moon, Daniel and I found a moment of peace. We stood at the edge of the village, gazing at the stars twinkling above.

"Olivia," Daniel said softly, "we've faced tremendous challenges, and we've always emerged stronger. This threat is formidable, but I have faith in us. The light of the Guardians will guide us."

I smiled, feeling gratitude and pride. "Thank you, Daniel. Our bond is our greatest strength. Together, we can face anything."

He held my hand, his touch warm and reassuring. "We'll build a future filled with hope and promise. Our love will carry us through whatever lies ahead."

As we stood together, bathed in the starlight, I made a silent vow. We would protect our world, no matter the cost. With the strength of our community and the deepening bond between us, we would confront the Whisper of Shadows and forge a future filled with promise.

The legacy of the Guardians would continue to shine, lighting our way through the darkness. And together, we would face the new threat with unwavering unity and determination.

### **CHAPTER 23: THE Gathering Storm**

As dawn broke over Ravenswood, our village lay in a tense yet resolute calm. The final battle with the Whisper of Shadows had been fought, but we knew that it had only been a temporary reprieve. The darkness still loomed, and we had to stay vigilant. Our unity and determination were our greatest weapons, and we would need them now more than ever.

In the days that followed, we focused on healing and rebuilding. The village was a hive of activity, with everyone working together to repair the damage and strengthen our defenses. The power of the Guardians continued to guide us, their wisdom and light a constant presence. Our friends and allies rallied with renewed determination, their resolve unwavering.

One evening, as the sun set and cast a warm golden light over the village, Clara convened a meeting in the council chamber. Her expression was one of determination and resolve, signaling that important decisions lay ahead.

"Everyone," Clara began, her voice steady and authoritative, "we have faced the Whisper of Shadows and held them at bay. But we must remain vigilant. The darkness is still a threat, and we need to be prepared for their return."

Lucas nodded, his eyes filled with resolve. "The Shadowstone has given us valuable insights, but we must continue to study its power and uncover any remaining secrets. Our knowledge will be our greatest asset in this ongoing battle."

Elara, ever the strategist, added, "We need to coordinate our efforts and ensure that our defenses are stronger than ever. The Whisper of Shadows will not stop until they have achieved their goal."

Alaric, exuding confidence, said, "I'll lead the efforts to fortify our borders and train our warriors. We cannot allow the darkness to gain a foothold."

Daniel, standing beside me, placed a reassuring hand on my shoulder. "We'll face this together, Olivia. Our bond is strong, and we can handle anything."

I took a deep breath, feeling the weight of the responsibility before us. "Let's do this. We'll protect our home and stand against the Whisper of Shadows."

THE DAYS TURNED INTO weeks as we worked tirelessly to strengthen our defenses and prepare for the next confrontation. The sense of unity and determination that had guided us through past challenges now fueled our resolve to protect our world from the Whisper of Shadows.

We fortified our borders, enhanced our magical protections, and trained our warriors with unwavering dedication. The power of the Guardians continued to guide us, their wisdom and light a constant presence. The sense of unity and camaraderie was palpable, and I could see the strength and resilience of our community shining through.

One evening, as the sun set and cast a warm golden light over the village, Daniel and I found a moment of quiet reflection. We stood at the edge of the village, gazing up at the stars, the night clear and filled with the gentle twinkle of constellations.

"Olivia," Daniel said softly, "we've faced tremendous challenges before, and we've always emerged stronger. This threat is formidable, but I have faith in us. The light of the Guardians will guide us."

I smiled, feeling gratitude and pride. "Thank you, Daniel. Our bond is our greatest strength. Together, we can face anything."

He held my hand, his touch warm and reassuring. "We'll build a future filled with hope and promise. Our love will carry us through whatever lies ahead."

THE NIGHT BEFORE THE anticipated return of the Whisper of Shadows, our forces gathered in the village square for a final council. The atmosphere was tense but filled with a sense of unity and determination. We knew that the battle ahead would be our greatest challenge yet.

Clara addressed the gathered crowd, her voice steady and authoritative. "Tomorrow, we face our greatest challenge. The Whisper of Shadows will return, and we must be prepared to defend our world. Our unity and strength will guide us through the battle ahead."

Lucas nodded in agreement. "The Shadowstone has given us valuable insights into their weaknesses. We must use this knowledge to our advantage and devise a strategy to defeat them once and for all."

Elara, ever the strategist, added, "We need to coordinate our efforts and ensure that our defenses are impenetrable. The Whisper of Shadows will not stop until they have achieved their goal."

Alaric, his presence radiating confidence, said, "I'll lead the charge. Our warriors are ready, and our defenses are strong. We will not let the darkness take hold."

Daniel, standing beside me, placed a reassuring hand on my shoulder. "We'll face this together, Olivia. Our bond is strong, and we can handle anything."

I took a deep breath, feeling the weight of the responsibility before us. "Let's do this. We'll protect our home and stand against the Whisper of Shadows."

THE MORNING OF THE battle arrived, and the village was alive with activity. Our forces prepared for the impending conflict with a sense of purpose and resolve. The air was thick with tension as we faced our enemies, our hearts pounding with a mixture of fear and determination.

The Whisper of Shadows' forces approached, their dark presence a stark contrast to the radiant light of our defenses. The sounds of combat echoed through the landscape as the battle began in earnest. Our unity and determination guided us through each clash, our resolve unwavering.

As the battle raged on, I felt the power of the Guardians surging within me. Drawing upon the energy of the Shadowstone, I channeled a brilliant beam of light that pierced through the darkness, striking the Whisper of Shadows' forces with precision.

The shadowy figures recoiled, their forms flickering and wavering. "You may have weakened us, Guardians, but you cannot defeat us. The darkness will always return."

With a final, desperate effort, the shadowy figure unleashed a powerful wave of dark energy that sent us sprawling. The ground trembled with the force of the attack, and the air crackled with tension. Yet, our unity and determination carried us through the onslaught, our resolve unshaken.

AS THE SUN SET AND cast a warm golden light over the battlefield, the sounds of combat began to wane. The Whisper of Shadows' forces were retreating, their presence a fading shadow in the light of our defenses. The battle was far from over, but our unity had carried us through another day.

That night, under the gentle light of the moon, Daniel and I found a moment of peace. We stood at the edge of the village, gazing at the stars twinkling above.

"Olivia," Daniel said softly, "we've faced tremendous challenges, and we've always emerged stronger. This threat is formidable, but I have faith in us. The light of the Guardians will guide us."

I smiled, feeling gratitude and pride. "Thank you, Daniel. Our bond is our greatest strength. Together, we can face anything."

He held my hand, his touch warm and reassuring. "We'll build a future filled with hope and promise. Our love will carry us through whatever lies ahead."

As we stood together, bathed in the starlight, I made a silent vow. We would protect our world, no matter the cost. With the strength of our community and the deepening bond between us, we would confront the Whisper of Shadows and forge a future filled with promise.

The legacy of the Guardians would continue to shine, lighting our way through the darkness. And together, we would face the new threat with unwavering unity and determination.

### **CHAPTER 24: SHADOWS' Last Stand**

The night had been long and tense, filled with the whispers of the coming storm. As dawn broke over Ravenswood, painting the sky in hues of pink and gold, the village stirred with a mixture of anticipation and determination. The final battle with the Whisper of Shadows was upon us, and our unity and strength would be tested like never before.

We gathered in the village square, our friends and allies standing shoulder to shoulder. The air was thick with a sense of purpose, and the resolve in our hearts was unyielding. We knew what was at stake, and we were prepared to fight for our home and our future.

Clara addressed the assembly, her voice strong and resolute. "Today, we face the Whisper of Shadows in their final stand. They seek to consume our world with darkness, but we will not let them prevail. Our unity and determination will guide us through this battle."

Lucas stepped forward, holding the Shadowstone aloft. "The power of the Shadowstone has revealed their weaknesses. We must use this knowledge to our advantage and strike at the heart of their darkness."

Elara, ever the strategist, added, "We will execute a multi-pronged attack. Our warriors will engage their forces head-on, while our mages and archers provide support from the flanks. We must stay united and fight with precision."

Alaric, exuding confidence, assured the group, "I'll lead the charge. Our warriors are ready, and our defenses are strong. We will not let the darkness take hold."

Daniel, standing beside me, placed a reassuring hand on my shoulder. "We'll face this together, Olivia. Our bond is our strength, and we can overcome anything."

I took a deep breath, feeling the weight of the responsibility before us. "Let's do this. We'll protect our home and stand against the Whisper of Shadows."

THE FINAL PREPARATIONS were swift and efficient. Our forces moved with purpose, their resolve unshaken. As the Whisper of Shadows' forces advanced, their dark presence a stark contrast to the light emanating from our defenses, the air crackled with anticipation.

The battle began with a deafening roar. The clash of light and darkness filled the air, the sounds of combat echoing through the landscape. Our forces engaged the enemy with precision, their movements a testament to their training and resolve.

The Whisper of Shadows' voice boomed through the battlefield, dripping with malice. "Guardians, you cannot escape the darkness. It will consume you."

Stepping forward with unwavering determination, I declared, "We will not let you harm our world. The unity and strength of our community will protect us."

The battle was fierce and chaotic. Our warriors fought with precision, their weapons gleaming in the light. Mages and archers provided crucial support, their spells and arrows striking true.

Throughout the conflict, I felt the power of the Guardians coursing through me. Drawing on the Shadowstone's energy, I unleashed a radiant beam of light, targeting the Whisper of Shadows' forces with pinpoint accuracy.

The shadowy figures recoiled, their forms flickering and wavering. "You may have weakened us, Guardians, but you cannot defeat us. The darkness will always return."

With a final, desperate effort, the Whisper of Shadows unleashed a powerful wave of dark energy that threatened to overwhelm us. The ground trembled, and the air crackled with tension. Yet, our unity and determination carried us through the onslaught, our resolve unwavering.

AS THE SUN SET, CASTING a warm golden light over the battlefield, the sounds of combat began to wane. The Whisper of Shadows' forces were in full retreat, their presence a fading shadow in the light of our defenses. The battle had been won, but the cost had been great.

Exhausted but triumphant, we gathered in the village square. The sense of relief and accomplishment was palpable. We had faced the darkness and emerged victorious, our unity and strength guiding us through the storm.

Clara addressed the assembled crowd, her voice filled with pride and gratitude. "Today, we have defended our world and protected our future. The darkness has been driven back, and the light of the Guardians will continue to shine."

Lucas nodded, his eyes filled with resolve. "The power of the Shadowstone and the wisdom of the Guardians have guided us to victory. We must continue to protect our world and ensure that the darkness never returns."

Elara, ever the strategist, added, "Our unity and determination have been our greatest strengths. We must continue to work together to build a future filled with hope and promise."

Alaric, his presence radiating confidence, said, "We have faced unimaginable challenges and emerged stronger. Our journey is far from over, but I know that together, we can handle anything."

Daniel, standing beside me, placed a reassuring hand on my shoulder. "Olivia, we have faced the darkness and won. Our bond is our strength, and together, we can face whatever lies ahead."

I smiled, feeling a deep sense of pride and gratitude. "Thank you, Daniel. Our bond has been our greatest strength. Together, we can build a future filled with hope and promise."

THAT NIGHT, UNDER THE gentle light of the moon, Daniel and I found a moment of peace. We stood at the edge of the village, gazing at the stars twinkling above.

"Olivia," Daniel said softly, "we've faced tremendous challenges, and we've always emerged stronger. This threat was formidable, but our unity and determination carried us through."

I smiled, feeling gratitude and pride. "Thank you, Daniel. Our bond is our greatest strength. Together, we can face anything."

He held my hand, his touch warm and reassuring. "We'll build a future filled with hope and promise. Our love will carry us through whatever lies ahead."

As we stood together, bathed in the starlight, I made a silent vow. We would protect our world, no matter the cost. With the strength of our community and the deepening bond between us, we would build a future filled with promise.

The legacy of the Guardians would continue to shine, lighting our way through the darkness. And together, we would face the new challenges with unwavering unity and determination.

### **CHAPTER 25: REBUILDING and Renewal**

The battle had been won, and the Whisper of Shadows had been driven back. The village of Ravenswood was filled with a sense of relief and triumph, but the cost of victory was evident. The damage from the conflict was extensive, and the scars of battle were visible on both the landscape and our hearts. Yet, amidst the wreckage and loss, there was a growing sense of hope and renewal. We had faced the darkness and emerged stronger, and now it was time to heal and rebuild.

As the first light of dawn broke over the horizon, casting a soft glow over the village, our community came together to begin the process of rebuilding. The air was filled with the sounds of activity as we worked to repair the damage and restore our home. The sense of unity and determination that had guided us through the battle now fueled our efforts to create a brighter future.

Clara, ever the voice of reason, coordinated the rebuilding efforts with efficiency and care. "We need to prioritize the repair of essential structures and ensure that everyone has a safe place to stay. Our strength lies in our unity, and we must support each other in this time of need."

Lucas and Elara, with their combined knowledge and strategic minds, devised plans to strengthen our defenses and protect our village from future threats. "The insights from the Shadowstone have given us valuable knowledge," Lucas said. "We must use this wisdom to create a safe and secure environment for our community."

Alaric led the efforts to train new warriors and enhance our magical protections. "We cannot become complacent," he reminded us. "The darkness may have been driven back, but we must remain vigilant and prepared."

Daniel, standing beside me, offered his unwavering support and encouragement. "Olivia, we've faced the darkness and won. Our bond is our strength, and together, we can build a future filled with hope and promise."

I smiled, feeling a deep sense of pride and gratitude. "Thank you, Daniel. Our bond has been our greatest strength. Together, we can overcome any challenge."

IN THE WEEKS THAT FOLLOWED, our village began to flourish once more. Homes were rebuilt, fields were replanted, and the sounds of laughter and life returned to the streets. The sense of hope and renewal was palpable, and it filled our hearts with gratitude and determination.

Our friends and allies continued to work together, their unity and resilience shining through. Schools and training centers flourished, passing on the teachings of the Guardians to the next generation. The power of the artifacts we had collected was carefully guarded, their energy used to support and protect our world.

One evening, as the sun set and cast a warm golden light over the village, Daniel and I found a moment of quiet reflection. We stood at the edge of the village, gazing up at the stars, the night clear and filled with the gentle twinkle of constellations.

"Olivia," Daniel said softly, "we've come so far together. Our journey has been filled with challenges and triumphs, and I am so proud of everything we've accomplished."

I smiled, feeling a deep sense of contentment. "Thank you, Daniel. Our bond has been our greatest strength. Together, we can face anything."

He took my hand, his touch warm and reassuring. "We'll continue to build a future filled with hope and promise. Our love will guide us through whatever challenges lie ahead."

AS THE SEASONS CHANGED, bringing new challenges and opportunities, our community continued to thrive. The sense of unity and resilience that had guided us through the darkest times now fueled our efforts to build a brighter future. The bonds we had forged in battle remained unbreakable, and our commitment to protecting our world was unwavering.

The ancient texts and artifacts we had collected provided invaluable knowledge and wisdom, guiding our efforts to restore and protect our world. We established new alliances and strengthened existing ones, ensuring that our community remained strong and united.

Alaric's efforts to secure our borders and protect our communities proved invaluable. Watchtowers and patrols ensured that any potential threats were swiftly dealt with, and the sense of safety and security allowed our communities to flourish.

Clara and Lucas's research continued to uncover new insights and strategies to protect our world. Their dedication to understanding the power of the Guardians and the balance between light and darkness guided our efforts to create a harmonious and just society.

Elara's strategic mind remained a guiding force in our efforts to rebuild and strengthen our communities. Her leadership and vision helped us navigate the challenges of growth and change, ensuring that our resources were used efficiently and effectively.

Through it all, the bond between us remained unbreakable. Daniel, Clara, Lucas, Elara, Alaric, and I stood side by side, our unity and determination guiding us through each step. The strength and resilience of our community were a testament to the power of unity and the enduring light within us.

ONE EVENING, AS THE sun set and cast a warm golden light over the village, we gathered in the town square to celebrate the annual Festival of Light. The air was filled with the sounds of laughter and music, and the scent of delicious food wafted through the streets. The festival was a time to reflect on our journey, celebrate our achievements, and look forward to the future.

As I stood on the stage, addressing the gathered crowd, I felt a deep sense of pride and gratitude. "Tonight, we celebrate the light within us and the unity that has brought us here. We have faced darkness and emerged stronger. Our communities are thriving, and the legacy of the Guardians continues to guide us."

The crowd erupted in cheers, their faces filled with joy and hope. The sense of camaraderie and mutual support was palpable, and I could see the strength and resilience of our people shining through.

Daniel, Clara, Lucas, Elara, and Alaric joined me on the stage, their presence a testament to the bonds we had forged and the journey we had undertaken. Together, we looked out at the faces of our friends and allies, our hearts filled with hope and determination.

AS THE FESTIVAL CONTINUED, I found a moment of quiet reflection, standing at the edge of the village and gazing up at the stars. The night was clear, and the constellations seemed to twinkle with a gentle, comforting light. I felt the presence of the Guardians, their wisdom and strength a constant guide.

Daniel joined me, his presence a comforting balm to my soul. "Olivia, you have been our guiding light. Your strength and determination have inspired us all. Together, we will continue to build a future filled with hope and promise."

I smiled, feeling a deep sense of pride and gratitude. "Thank you, Daniel. Our bond has been our greatest strength. Together, we can face anything."

He took my hand, his touch warm and reassuring. "Our journey is far from over, but I know that we can handle whatever comes next. The light of the Guardians will continue to guide us, illuminating the path to a brighter tomorrow."

As we stood together, the gentle light of the stars casting a soothing glow over the village, I made a silent vow. We would continue to protect our world, no matter the cost. With the strength and resilience of our community, and the deepening bond between us, we would face

whatever challenges lay ahead and build a future filled with promise and possibility.

The legacy of the Guardians would continue to shine, guiding us through the darkness and illuminating the path to a brighter tomorrow. And together, we would build a world filled with hope, unity, and endless possibilities.

### **CHAPTER 26: THE Guardians' Legacy**

The battle against the Whisper of Shadows had been a defining moment for our community. We had faced the darkness head-on and emerged victorious. Now, as the village of Ravenswood continued to heal and rebuild, we looked toward the future with a sense of hope and determination. The legacy of the Guardians would guide us as we forged a path forward.

As the seasons changed, the village flourished. Homes were restored, fields thrived, and the sounds of daily life returned to the streets. The sense of unity and resilience that had carried us through the darkest times now fueled our efforts to create a brighter future. The bonds we had forged in battle remained unbreakable, and our commitment to protecting our world was unwavering.

One crisp autumn morning, as the leaves turned vibrant shades of red and gold, Daniel and I stood at the edge of the village, reflecting on the journey that had brought us here. The air was cool, and the scent of pine and earth filled our senses. I felt a profound connection to the land and the people who had fought to protect it.

"Olivia," Daniel began, his voice filled with warmth and affection, "look at how far we've come. Our world is thriving, and our communities are stronger than ever. It's because of you."

I smiled, feeling a deep sense of pride and gratitude. "It's because of all of us, Daniel. Our unity and determination have brought us here. We've faced unimaginable challenges, and we've overcome them together."

He took my hand, his touch warm and reassuring. "Our journey is far from over, but I know that together, we can handle whatever comes next. The light of the Guardians will continue to guide us, illuminating the path to a brighter tomorrow."

IN THE MONTHS THAT followed, our efforts to strengthen our community and protect our world continued. Schools and training centers flourished, passing on the teachings of the Guardians to the next generation. The power of the artifacts we had collected was carefully guarded, their energy used to support and protect our world.

Alaric's efforts to secure our borders and protect our communities proved invaluable. Watchtowers and patrols ensured that any potential threats were swiftly dealt with, and the sense of safety and security allowed our communities to thrive.

Clara and Lucas's research continued to uncover new insights and strategies to protect our world. Their dedication to understanding the power of the Guardians and the balance between light and darkness guided our efforts to create a harmonious and just society.

Elara's strategic mind remained a guiding force in our efforts to rebuild and strengthen our communities. Her leadership and vision helped us navigate the challenges of growth and change, ensuring that our resources were used efficiently and effectively.

Through it all, the bond between us remained unbreakable. Daniel, Clara, Lucas, Elara, Alaric, and I stood side by side, our unity and determination guiding us through each step. The strength and resilience of our community were a testament to the power of unity and the enduring light within us.

ONE EVENING, AS THE sun set and cast a warm golden light over the village, we gathered in the town square to celebrate the Festival of Unity. The air was filled with the sounds of laughter and music, and the scent of delicious food wafted through the streets. The festival was a time to reflect on our journey, celebrate our achievements, and look forward to the future.

As I stood on the stage, addressing the gathered crowd, I felt a deep sense of pride and gratitude. "Tonight, we celebrate the unity that has brought us here. We have faced darkness and emerged stronger. Our communities are thriving, and the legacy of the Guardians continues to guide us."

The crowd erupted in cheers, their faces filled with joy and hope. The sense of camaraderie and mutual support was palpable, and I could see the strength and resilience of our people shining through.

Daniel, Clara, Lucas, Elara, and Alaric joined me on the stage, their presence a testament to the bonds we had forged and the journey we had undertaken. Together, we looked out at the faces of our friends and allies, our hearts filled with hope and determination.

AS THE FESTIVAL CONTINUED, I found a moment of quiet reflection, standing at the edge of the village and gazing up at the stars. The night was clear, and the constellations seemed to twinkle with a gentle, comforting light. I felt the presence of the Guardians, their wisdom and strength a constant guide.

Daniel joined me, his presence a comforting balm to my soul. "Olivia, you have been our guiding light. Your strength and determination have inspired us all. Together, we will continue to build a future filled with hope and promise."

I smiled, feeling a deep sense of pride and gratitude. "Thank you, Daniel. Our bond has been our greatest strength. Together, we can face anything."

He took my hand, his touch warm and reassuring. "Our journey is far from over, but I know that we can handle whatever comes next. The light of the Guardians will continue to guide us, illuminating the path to a brighter tomorrow."

As we stood together, the gentle light of the stars casting a soothing glow over the village, I made a silent vow. We would continue to protect our world, no matter the cost. With the strength and resilience of our community, and the deepening bond between us, we would face whatever challenges lay ahead and build a future filled with promise and possibility.

The legacy of the Guardians would continue to shine, guiding us through the darkness and illuminating the path to a brighter tomorrow. And together, we would build a world filled with hope, unity, and endless possibilities.

### **CHAPTER 27: A NEW Chapter Begins**

The whispers of war had faded, and the village of Ravenswood was thriving once more. The unity and strength that had seen us through our darkest days now fueled our journey into a new era. As our community healed and grew, we remained steadfast in our commitment to protect our world and honor the legacy of the Guardians.

One crisp winter morning, as snowflakes danced in the air and the ground lay blanketed in a soft layer of snow, Daniel and I walked through the village, taking in the serene beauty of the landscape. The cold air was refreshing, and the sense of peace and renewal filled our hearts with gratitude.

"Olivia," Daniel said, his breath visible in the chilly air, "it's incredible to see how far we've come. The village is thriving, and our community is stronger than ever. This is all because of you."

I smiled, feeling a deep sense of pride and warmth. "It's because of all of us, Daniel. Our unity and determination have brought us here. We've faced unimaginable challenges, and we've overcome them together."

He squeezed my hand, his touch a comforting presence. "And we'll continue to face whatever comes next together. The light of the Guardians will always guide us, illuminating our path forward."

AS THE DAYS GREW SHORTER and the winter deepened, our efforts to strengthen our community and protect our world continued. Schools and training centers remained bustling hubs of activity, passing on the teachings of the Guardians to the next generation. The power of the artifacts we had collected was carefully guarded, their energy used to support and protect our world.

Alaric's efforts to secure our borders and protect our communities proved invaluable. Watchtowers and patrols ensured that any potential threats were swiftly addressed, and the sense of safety and security allowed our communities to flourish.

Clara and Lucas's research continued to uncover new insights and strategies to protect our world. Their dedication to understanding the power of the Guardians and the balance between light and darkness guided our efforts to create a harmonious and just society.

Elara's strategic mind remained a guiding force in our efforts to rebuild and strengthen our communities. Her leadership and vision helped us navigate the challenges of growth and change, ensuring that our resources were used efficiently and effectively.

Through it all, the bond between us remained unbreakable. Daniel, Clara, Lucas, Elara, Alaric, and I stood side by side, our unity and determination guiding us through each step. The strength and resilience of our community were a testament to the power of unity and the enduring light within us.

ONE EVENING, AS THE sun set and cast a warm golden light over the snow-covered village, we gathered in the town square to celebrate the Winter Solstice Festival. The air was filled with the sounds of laughter and music, and the scent of delicious food wafted through the streets. The festival was a time to reflect on our journey, celebrate our achievements, and look forward to the future.

As I stood on the stage, addressing the gathered crowd, I felt a deep sense of pride and gratitude. "Tonight, we celebrate the unity that has brought us here. We have faced darkness and emerged stronger. Our communities are thriving, and the legacy of the Guardians continues to guide us."

The crowd erupted in cheers, their faces filled with joy and hope. The sense of camaraderie and mutual support was palpable, and I could see the strength and resilience of our people shining through.

Daniel, Clara, Lucas, Elara, and Alaric joined me on the stage, their presence a testament to the bonds we had forged and the journey we had undertaken. Together, we looked out at the faces of our friends and allies, our hearts filled with hope and determination.

AS THE FESTIVAL CONTINUED, I found a moment of quiet reflection, standing at the edge of the village and gazing up at the stars. The night was clear, and the constellations seemed to twinkle with a gentle, comforting light. I felt the presence of the Guardians, their wisdom and strength a constant guide.

Daniel joined me, his presence a comforting balm to my soul. "Olivia, you have been our guiding light. Your strength and determination have inspired us all. Together, we will continue to build a future filled with hope and promise."

I smiled, feeling a deep sense of pride and gratitude. "Thank you, Daniel. Our bond has been our greatest strength. Together, we can face anything."

He took my hand, his touch warm and reassuring. "Our journey is far from over, but I know that we can handle whatever comes next. The light of the Guardians will continue to guide us, illuminating the path to a brighter tomorrow."

As we stood together, the gentle light of the stars casting a soothing glow over the village, I made a silent vow. We would continue to protect our world, no matter the cost. With the strength and resilience of our community, and the deepening bond between us, we would face whatever challenges lay ahead and build a future filled with promise and possibility.

The legacy of the Guardians would continue to shine, guiding us through the darkness and illuminating the path to a brighter tomorrow. And together, we would build a world filled with hope, unity, and endless possibilities.

### **CHAPTER 28: A NEW Chapter Begins**

The joy and celebration of our wedding lingered in the air, filling Ravenswood with a renewed sense of hope and unity. The bonds we had forged through trials and triumphs were stronger than ever, and the legacy of the Guardians continued to guide us as we moved forward. The village, now thriving, was a testament to our resilience and determination.

As winter gave way to spring, the village was transformed by the warmth and light of the new season. Flowers bloomed, fields turned green, and the sounds of life returned to the streets. The energy of renewal and growth was palpable, and it filled our hearts with a sense of anticipation for the future.

One sunny morning, as Daniel and I walked through the blossoming fields, we talked about our dreams and aspirations for the future. The scent of fresh flowers filled the air, and the gentle breeze carried with it a sense of promise and possibility.

"Olivia," Daniel began, his voice filled with warmth and determination, "our journey together has been incredible, but I feel there's so much more we can achieve. I want to explore new horizons and discover new ways to protect and strengthen our world."

I smiled, feeling a deep sense of excitement and curiosity. "I agree, Daniel. There's a whole world out there, filled with opportunities and challenges. Together, we can make a difference and continue to build on the legacy of the Guardians."

He took my hand, his touch a comforting presence. "Let's embark on this new journey together. We'll face whatever comes next with the same unity and determination that has always guided us."

IN THE MONTHS THAT followed, Daniel and I began to explore new avenues for growth and development. We traveled to neighboring villages and towns, forging new alliances and sharing the knowledge and wisdom we had gained. The sense of unity and collaboration was strong, and it filled us with hope for the future.

Alaric continued to lead the efforts to secure our borders and protect our communities. His unwavering dedication and strategic mind ensured that Ravenswood remained safe and secure.

Clara and Lucas's research continued to uncover new insights into the power of the Guardians and the balance between light and darkness. Their discoveries guided our efforts to create a harmonious and just society.

Elara's leadership and vision helped us navigate the challenges of growth and change. Her strategic mind and careful planning ensured that our resources were used efficiently and effectively.

Through it all, the bond between us remained unbreakable. Daniel, Clara, Lucas, Elara, Alaric, and I stood side by side, our unity and determination guiding us through each step. The strength and resilience of our community were a testament to the power of unity and the enduring light within us.

ONE EVENING, AS THE sun set and cast a warm golden light over the village, we gathered in the town square to celebrate the Festival of Renewal. The air was filled with the sounds of laughter and music, and the scent of delicious food wafted through the streets. The festival was a time to reflect on our journey, celebrate our achievements, and look forward to the future.

As I stood on the stage, addressing the gathered crowd, I felt a deep sense of pride and gratitude. "Tonight, we celebrate the renewal and growth that has brought us here. We have faced darkness and emerged stronger. Our communities are thriving, and the legacy of the Guardians continues to guide us."

The crowd erupted in cheers, their faces filled with joy and hope. The sense of camaraderie and mutual support was palpable, and I could see the strength and resilience of our people shining through.

Daniel, Clara, Lucas, Elara, and Alaric joined me on the stage, their presence a testament to the bonds we had forged and the journey we had undertaken. Together, we looked out at the faces of our friends and allies, our hearts filled with hope and determination.

AS THE FESTIVAL CONTINUED, I found a moment of quiet reflection, standing at the edge of the village and gazing up at the stars. The night was clear, and the constellations seemed to twinkle with

a gentle, comforting light. I felt the presence of the Guardians, their wisdom and strength a constant guide.

Daniel joined me, his presence a comforting balm to my soul. "Olivia, you have been our guiding light. Your strength and determination have inspired us all. Together, we will continue to build a future filled with hope and promise."

I smiled, feeling a deep sense of pride and gratitude. "Thank you, Daniel. Our bond has been our greatest strength. Together, we can face anything."

He took my hand, his touch warm and reassuring. "Our journey is far from over, but I know that we can handle whatever comes next. The light of the Guardians will continue to guide us, illuminating the path to a brighter tomorrow."

As we stood together, the gentle light of the stars casting a soothing glow over the village, I made a silent vow. We would continue to protect our world, no matter the cost. With the strength and resilience of our community, and the deepening bond between us, we would face whatever challenges lay ahead and build a future filled with promise and possibility.

The legacy of the Guardians would continue to shine, guiding us through the darkness and illuminating the path to a brighter tomorrow. And together, we would build a world filled with hope, unity, and endless possibilities.

### **CHAPTER 29: THE Winds of Change**

The joy and celebration of our wedding lingered in the air, filling Ravenswood with a renewed sense of hope and unity. The bonds we had forged through trials and triumphs were stronger than ever, and the legacy of the Guardians continued to guide us as we moved forward. The village, now thriving, was a testament to our resilience and determination.

As winter gave way to spring, the village was transformed by the warmth and light of the new season. Flowers bloomed, fields turned green, and the sounds of life returned to the streets. The energy of renewal and growth was palpable, and it filled our hearts with a sense of anticipation for the future.

One sunny morning, as Daniel and I walked through the blossoming fields, we talked about our dreams and aspirations for the future. The scent of fresh flowers filled the air, and the gentle breeze carried with it a sense of promise and possibility.

"Olivia," Daniel began, his voice filled with warmth and determination, "our journey together has been incredible, but I feel there's so much more we can achieve. I want to explore new horizons and discover new ways to protect and strengthen our world."

I smiled, feeling a deep sense of excitement and curiosity. "I agree, Daniel. There's a whole world out there, filled with opportunities and challenges. Together, we can make a difference and continue to build on the legacy of the Guardians."

He took my hand, his touch a comforting presence. "Let's embark on this new journey together. We'll face whatever comes next with the same unity and determination that has always guided us."

IN THE MONTHS THAT followed, Daniel and I began to explore new avenues for growth and development. We traveled to neighboring villages and towns, forging new alliances and sharing the knowledge and wisdom we had gained. The sense of unity and collaboration was strong, and it filled us with hope for the future.

Alaric continued to lead the efforts to secure our borders and protect our communities. His unwavering dedication and strategic mind ensured that Ravenswood remained safe and secure.

Clara and Lucas's research continued to uncover new insights into the power of the Guardians and the balance between light and darkness. Their discoveries guided our efforts to create a harmonious and just society.

Elara's leadership and vision helped us navigate the challenges of growth and change. Her strategic mind and careful planning ensured that our resources were used efficiently and effectively.

Through it all, the bond between us remained unbreakable. Daniel, Clara, Lucas, Elara, Alaric, and I stood side by side, our unity and determination guiding us through each step. The strength and resilience of our community were a testament to the power of unity and the enduring light within us.

ONE EVENING, AS THE sun set and cast a warm golden light over the village, we gathered in the town square to celebrate the Festival of Renewal. The air was filled with the sounds of laughter and music, and the scent of delicious food wafted through the streets. The festival was a time to reflect on our journey, celebrate our achievements, and look forward to the future.

As I stood on the stage, addressing the gathered crowd, I felt a deep sense of pride and gratitude. "Tonight, we celebrate the renewal and growth that has brought us here. We have faced darkness and emerged stronger. Our communities are thriving, and the legacy of the Guardians continues to guide us."

The crowd erupted in cheers, their faces filled with joy and hope. The sense of camaraderie and mutual support was palpable, and I could see the strength and resilience of our people shining through.

Daniel, Clara, Lucas, Elara, and Alaric joined me on the stage, their presence a testament to the bonds we had forged and the journey we had undertaken. Together, we looked out at the faces of our friends and allies, our hearts filled with hope and determination.

AS THE FESTIVAL CONTINUED, I found a moment of quiet reflection, standing at the edge of the village and gazing up at the stars. The night was clear, and the constellations seemed to twinkle with a gentle, comforting light. I felt the presence of the Guardians, their wisdom and strength a constant guide.

Daniel joined me, his presence a comforting balm to my soul. "Olivia, you have been our guiding light. Your strength and determination have inspired us all. Together, we will continue to build a future filled with hope and promise."

I smiled, feeling a deep sense of pride and gratitude. "Thank you, Daniel. Our bond has been our greatest strength. Together, we can face anything."

He took my hand, his touch warm and reassuring. "Our journey is far from over, but I know that we can handle whatever comes next. The light of the Guardians will continue to guide us, illuminating the path to a brighter tomorrow."

As we stood together, the gentle light of the stars casting a soothing glow over the village, I made a silent vow. We would continue to protect our world, no matter the cost. With the strength and resilience of our community, and the deepening bond between us, we would face whatever challenges lay ahead and build a future filled with promise and possibility.

The legacy of the Guardians would continue to shine, guiding us through the darkness and illuminating the path to a brighter tomorrow. And together, we would build a world filled with hope, unity, and endless possibilities.

### **CHAPTER 30: THE Legacy Continues**

The village of Ravenswood thrived under the warmth of the spring sun, a testament to the resilience and unity that had seen us through countless trials. The bonds forged through battles and triumphs had grown ever stronger, and the legacy of the Guardians continued to light our path. As our community looked toward the future, we remained steadfast in our commitment to protect our world and build a brighter tomorrow.

One afternoon, as the fields were alive with the vibrant colors of blooming flowers, Daniel and I walked hand in hand through the village, reflecting on the journey that had brought us here. The scent of fresh blossoms filled the air, and the gentle breeze carried with it a sense of peace and renewal.

"Olivia," Daniel began, his voice filled with warmth and resolve, "our journey together has been extraordinary, but I feel there's still so much more we can achieve. I believe it's time to pass on our knowledge and ensure that the legacy of the Guardians continues to thrive."

I smiled, feeling a deep sense of purpose and excitement. "I agree, Daniel. The next generation needs to understand the importance of unity and resilience. Let's focus on mentoring and guiding them so they can carry forward the light of the Guardians."

He squeezed my hand, his touch a comforting presence. "Let's embark on this new chapter together. We'll face whatever comes next with the same determination and unity that has always guided us."

IN THE MONTHS THAT followed, Daniel and I dedicated ourselves to mentoring the younger members of our community. We established new training programs and workshops, passing on the knowledge and wisdom we had gained. The sense of unity and collaboration was strong, and it filled us with hope for the future.

Alaric continued to lead the efforts to secure our borders and protect our communities. His unwavering dedication and strategic mind ensured that Ravenswood remained safe and secure.

Clara and Lucas's research continued to uncover new insights into the power of the Guardians and the balance between light and darkness. Their discoveries guided our efforts to create a harmonious and just society.

Elara's leadership and vision helped us navigate the challenges of growth and change. Her strategic mind and careful planning ensured that our resources were used efficiently and effectively.

Through it all, the bond between us remained unbreakable. Daniel, Clara, Lucas, Elara, Alaric, and I stood side by side, our unity and determination guiding us through each step. The strength and resilience of our community were a testament to the power of unity and the enduring light within us.

ONE EVENING, AS THE sun set and cast a warm golden light over the village, we gathered in the town square to celebrate the Festival of Guardians. The air was filled with the sounds of laughter and music, and the scent of delicious food wafted through the streets. The festival was a time to reflect on our journey, celebrate our achievements, and look forward to the future.

As I stood on the stage, addressing the gathered crowd, I felt a deep sense of pride and gratitude. "Tonight, we celebrate the legacy of the Guardians and the unity that has brought us here. We have faced darkness and emerged stronger. Our communities are thriving, and the light of the Guardians continues to guide us."

The crowd erupted in cheers, their faces filled with joy and hope. The sense of camaraderie and mutual support was palpable, and I could see the strength and resilience of our people shining through.

Daniel, Clara, Lucas, Elara, and Alaric joined me on the stage, their presence a testament to the bonds we had forged and the journey we had undertaken. Together, we looked out at the faces of our friends and allies, our hearts filled with hope and determination.

AS THE FESTIVAL CONTINUED, I found a moment of quiet reflection, standing at the edge of the village and gazing up at the stars. The night was clear, and the constellations seemed to twinkle with a gentle, comforting light. I felt the presence of the Guardians, their wisdom and strength a constant guide.

Daniel joined me, his presence a comforting balm to my soul. "Olivia, you have been our guiding light. Your strength and determination have inspired us all. Together, we will continue to build a future filled with hope and promise."

I smiled, feeling a deep sense of pride and gratitude. "Thank you, Daniel. Our bond has been our greatest strength. Together, we can face anything."

He took my hand, his touch warm and reassuring. "Our journey is far from over, but I know that we can handle whatever comes next. The light of the Guardians will continue to guide us, illuminating the path to a brighter tomorrow."

As we stood together, the gentle light of the stars casting a soothing glow over the village, I made a silent vow. We would continue to protect our world, no matter the cost. With the strength and resilience of our community, and the deepening bond between us, we would face whatever challenges lay ahead and build a future filled with promise and possibility.

The legacy of the Guardians would continue to shine, guiding us through the darkness and illuminating the path to a brighter tomorrow. And together, we would build a world filled with hope, unity, and endless possibilities.

### **CHAPTER 34: ECHOES of the Past**

As the summer days continued to bring warmth and light to Ravenswood, the village buzzed with activity and the promise of new beginnings. The unity and strength that had carried us through countless challenges now flourished in the vibrant energy of the season. The bonds we had forged were unbreakable, and the legacy of the Guardians continued to inspire and guide us.

One afternoon, as Daniel and I explored the outskirts of the village, we came across an old, overgrown path that led into the heart of the forest. The path was seldom traveled, and curiosity sparked within us as we decided to follow it.

"Olivia," Daniel said, his voice filled with excitement and wonder, "I've never seen this path before. It looks like it hasn't been used in years. Let's see where it leads."

I nodded, feeling a sense of adventure and anticipation. "Let's go. Who knows what we might discover?"

As we walked along the narrow, winding path, the trees grew denser, and the air was filled with the scent of pine and earth. The sunlight filtered through the canopy, casting dappled shadows on the forest floor. The sense of history and mystery grew stronger with each step.

After a while, we emerged into a small clearing, where we found the remnants of an ancient stone structure. The ruins were covered in moss and vines, and the air was thick with the whispers of the past. It was a place that seemed to hold secrets and stories long forgotten.

"Daniel, look at this," I said, my voice filled with awe. "These ruins must have been here for centuries. I wonder what they were used for."

He approached the stone structure, examining the intricate carvings and symbols etched into the weathered stone. "These symbols look familiar, Olivia. They remind me of the markings we've seen on the artifacts and the Shadowstone. This place could be connected to the Guardians."

A sense of excitement and curiosity filled me as we continued to explore the ruins. The carvings and symbols seemed to tell a story, and I felt a deep connection to the history of the place. It was as if the echoes of the past were calling out to us, urging us to uncover their secrets.

OVER THE NEXT FEW DAYS, we returned to the ruins with Clara, Lucas, Elara, and Alaric. Together, we began to study the symbols and carvings, seeking to uncover the hidden knowledge and history of the ancient structure. The sense of camaraderie and shared purpose was palpable, and we worked tirelessly to decipher the clues left by our ancestors.

Clara's expertise in ancient languages and symbols proved invaluable as she translated the inscriptions. "These carvings speak of a time when the Guardians first established their order. It seems that this place was a sanctuary, a place of learning and meditation for the early Guardians."

Lucas nodded in agreement. "The artifacts and symbols we've found here are consistent with what we've seen in other ancient sites. This place could hold important knowledge about the origins of the Guardians and their teachings."

Elara, ever the strategist, added, "We should document everything we find and continue our research. This sanctuary could provide valuable insights into the history and wisdom of the Guardians."

Alaric's eyes gleamed with determination. "I'll oversee the excavation and ensure that everything is handled with care. This place is a treasure trove of knowledge, and we must protect it."

AS WE CONTINUED OUR research and exploration, we uncovered more and more about the history of the Guardians and their early teachings. The sense of connection to the past was profound, and it filled us with a renewed sense of purpose and determination.

One evening, as the sun set and cast a warm golden light over the ancient ruins, Daniel and I found a moment of quiet reflection. We stood in the clearing, gazing at the weathered stones and the intricate carvings that told the story of our ancestors.

"Olivia," Daniel said softly, "this place is a testament to the strength and wisdom of the Guardians. Their legacy continues to guide us, and it's our responsibility to honor and preserve it."

I smiled, feeling a deep sense of pride and gratitude. "Thank you, Daniel. Our bond and our connection to the Guardians have been our greatest strengths. Together, we can continue to protect our world and build a future filled with hope and promise."

He took my hand, his touch warm and reassuring. "We'll continue to uncover the secrets of the past and use that knowledge to guide us into the future. The light of the Guardians will continue to illuminate our path, just as it always has."

As we stood together, the gentle light of the stars casting a soothing glow over the ruins, I made a silent vow. We would continue to protect our world, no matter the cost. With the strength and resilience of our community, and the deepening bond between us, we would face whatever challenges lay ahead and build a future filled with promise and possibility.

The legacy of the Guardians would continue to shine, guiding us through the darkness and illuminating the path to a brighter tomorrow. And together, we would build a world filled with hope, unity, and endless possibilities.

### **CHAPTER 35: THE Wisdom of Ages**

The discovery of the ancient ruins had breathed new life into our quest for knowledge and understanding. The secrets and wisdom of the Guardians' past were now within our reach, and the sense of purpose and determination in Ravenswood had never been stronger. The village buzzed with excitement as we continued our exploration and research, driven by the desire to uncover the mysteries of the ancient sanctuary.

One morning, as the sun cast its golden light over the village, Daniel and I met with the council of Guardians to discuss our progress and plan our next steps. The council chamber was filled with an air of anticipation, and the faces of the council members reflected their dedication and resolve.

"Olivia, Daniel," Clara began, her voice steady and authoritative, "our research has already yielded valuable insights into the early teachings of the Guardians. However, there is still much more to uncover. We need to continue our exploration and ensure that we document everything we find."

Lucas nodded in agreement. "The symbols and inscriptions we've found provide a glimpse into the wisdom of the past. We must study them carefully and use that knowledge to guide our efforts in the present and future."

Elara, ever the strategist, added, "We should also focus on preserving the integrity of the ruins. This place is a treasure trove of knowledge, and we must ensure that it remains intact for future generations to study and learn from."

Alaric, his presence radiating confidence, said, "I'll oversee the excavation and ensure that everything is handled with care. We cannot afford to make any mistakes."

Daniel, standing beside me, placed a reassuring hand on my shoulder. "We'll face this together, Olivia. Our bond is our strength, and we can overcome any challenge."

I took a deep breath, feeling the weight of the responsibility before us. "Let's do this. We'll continue to uncover the secrets of the past and use that knowledge to build a future filled with hope and promise."

IN THE DAYS THAT FOLLOWED, the village of Ravenswood was a hive of activity. The council of Guardians and our team of researchers worked tirelessly to document and study the symbols and inscriptions found in the ancient ruins. The sense of unity and collaboration was strong, and it filled us with hope for the future.

Clara's expertise in ancient languages and symbols proved invaluable as she continued to translate the inscriptions. "These carvings speak of the early Guardians' dedication to balance and harmony. Their teachings emphasize the importance of unity, compassion, and wisdom."

Lucas nodded in agreement. "The artifacts we've found here also suggest that the early Guardians were skilled in both magic and practical knowledge. They sought to use their abilities to protect and nurture their communities."

Elara's strategic mind helped us plan our excavation and preservation efforts. "We need to be thorough and methodical in our approach. Each discovery could provide valuable insights into the history and wisdom of the Guardians."

Alaric's leadership ensured that our efforts were carried out with care and precision. "We'll take every precaution to preserve the integrity of the ruins. This place is a testament to the strength and wisdom of the Guardians, and we must honor and protect it."

AS WE CONTINUED OUR research and exploration, we uncovered more about the history of the Guardians and their early teachings. The sense of connection to the past was profound, and it filled us with a renewed sense of purpose and determination.

One evening, as the sun set and cast a warm golden light over the ancient ruins, Daniel and I found a moment of quiet reflection. We stood in the clearing, gazing at the weathered stones and the intricate carvings that told the story of our ancestors.

"Olivia," Daniel said softly, "this place is a testament to the strength and wisdom of the Guardians. Their legacy continues to guide us, and it's our responsibility to honor and preserve it."

I smiled, feeling a deep sense of pride and gratitude. "Thank you, Daniel. Our bond and our connection to the Guardians have been our greatest strengths. Together, we can continue to protect our world and build a future filled with hope and promise."

He took my hand, his touch warm and reassuring. "We'll continue to uncover the secrets of the past and use that knowledge to guide us into the future. The light of the Guardians will continue to illuminate our path, just as it always has."

AS THE WEEKS TURNED into months, our efforts to uncover the secrets of the ancient ruins continued. The knowledge we gained provided valuable insights into the early teachings of the Guardians and guided our efforts to create a harmonious and just society.

One evening, as the sun set and cast a warm golden light over the village, we gathered in the town square to celebrate the Festival of Wisdom. The air was filled with the sounds of laughter and music, and the scent of delicious food wafted through the streets. The festival was a time to reflect on our journey, celebrate our achievements, and look forward to the future.

As I stood on the stage, addressing the gathered crowd, I felt a deep sense of pride and gratitude. "Tonight, we celebrate the wisdom and knowledge that have brought us here. We have faced darkness and emerged stronger. Our communities are thriving, and the legacy of the Guardians continues to guide us."

The crowd erupted in cheers, their faces filled with joy and hope. The sense of camaraderie and mutual support was palpable, and I could see the strength and resilience of our people shining through.

Daniel, Clara, Lucas, Elara, and Alaric joined me on the stage, their presence a testament to the bonds we had forged and the journey we had undertaken. Together, we looked out at the faces of our friends and allies, our hearts filled with hope and determination.

AS THE FESTIVAL CONTINUED, I found a moment of quiet reflection, standing at the edge of the village and gazing up at the stars. The night was clear, and the constellations seemed to twinkle with a gentle, comforting light. I felt the presence of the Guardians, their wisdom and strength a constant guide.

Daniel joined me, his presence a comforting balm to my soul. "Olivia, you have been our guiding light. Your strength and determination have inspired us all. Together, we will continue to build a future filled with hope and promise."

I smiled, feeling a deep sense of pride and gratitude. "Thank you, Daniel. Our bond has been our greatest strength. Together, we can face anything."

He took my hand, his touch warm and reassuring. "Our journey is far from over, but I know that we can handle whatever comes next. The light of the Guardians will continue to guide us, illuminating the path to a brighter tomorrow."

As we stood together, the gentle light of the stars casting a soothing glow over the village, I made a silent vow. We would continue to protect our world, no matter the cost. With the strength and resilience of our community, and the deepening bond between us, we would face whatever challenges lay ahead and build a future filled with promise and possibility.

The legacy of the Guardians would continue to shine, guiding us through the darkness and illuminating the path to a brighter tomorrow. And together, we would build a world filled with hope, unity, and endless possibilities.

### **CHAPTER 36: GUARDIANS' Unity**

The summer sun shone brightly over Ravenswood, infusing the village with warmth and the promise of new discoveries. Our journey to uncover the secrets of the ancient ruins had reignited our sense of purpose, and the legacy of the Guardians continued to inspire and guide us. The bonds we had forged were stronger than ever, and our community thrived under the guidance of the council of Guardians.

One clear morning, as the village buzzed with activity and the fields were lush with growth, Daniel and I gathered with the council to discuss the progress of our research and the next steps we needed to take. The council chamber was filled with an air of anticipation, and the faces of the council members reflected their dedication and resolve.

"Olivia, Daniel," Clara began, her voice steady and authoritative, "our research has uncovered significant insights into the early teachings of the Guardians. We now have a deeper understanding of their dedication to balance, harmony, and wisdom. However, there is still much more to learn. We need to continue our exploration and ensure that we preserve this knowledge for future generations."

Lucas nodded in agreement. "The symbols and inscriptions we've found are invaluable. We must study them carefully and use that knowledge to guide our efforts in the present and future."

Elara, ever the strategist, added, "We should also focus on sharing our discoveries with neighboring communities. The knowledge we've gained can help others strengthen their defenses and protect their worlds."

Alaric, his presence radiating confidence, said, "I'll oversee the preservation efforts and ensure that the ruins remain intact. We cannot afford to make any mistakes."

Daniel, standing beside me, placed a reassuring hand on my shoulder. "We'll face this together, Olivia. Our bond is our strength, and we can overcome any challenge."

I took a deep breath, feeling the weight of the responsibility before us. "Let's do this. We'll continue to uncover the secrets of the past and use that knowledge to build a future filled with hope and promise."

IN THE DAYS THAT FOLLOWED, the village of Ravenswood was a hive of activity. The council of Guardians and our team of researchers worked tirelessly to document and study the symbols and inscriptions found in the ancient ruins. The sense of unity and collaboration was strong, and it filled us with hope for the future.

Clara's expertise in ancient languages and symbols proved invaluable as she continued to translate the inscriptions. "These carvings speak of the early Guardians' commitment to unity and compassion. Their teachings emphasize the importance of working together and supporting one another."

Lucas nodded in agreement. "The artifacts we've found here also suggest that the early Guardians valued both magic and practical knowledge. They sought to use their abilities to protect and nurture their communities."

Elara's strategic mind helped us plan our excavation and preservation efforts. "We need to be thorough and methodical in our approach. Each discovery could provide valuable insights into the history and wisdom of the Guardians."

Alaric's leadership ensured that our efforts were carried out with care and precision. "We'll take every precaution to preserve the integrity of the ruins. This place is a testament to the strength and wisdom of the Guardians, and we must honor and protect it."

AS WE CONTINUED OUR research and exploration, we uncovered more about the history of the Guardians and their early teachings. The sense of connection to the past was profound, and it filled us with a renewed sense of purpose and determination.

One evening, as the sun set and cast a warm golden light over the ancient ruins, Daniel and I found a moment of quiet reflection. We stood in the clearing, gazing at the weathered stones and the intricate carvings that told the story of our ancestors.

"Olivia," Daniel said softly, "this place is a testament to the strength and wisdom of the Guardians. Their legacy continues to guide us, and it's our responsibility to honor and preserve it."

I smiled, feeling a deep sense of pride and gratitude. "Thank you, Daniel. Our bond and our connection to the Guardians have been our greatest strengths. Together, we can continue to protect our world and build a future filled with hope and promise."

He took my hand, his touch warm and reassuring. "We'll continue to uncover the secrets of the past and use that knowledge to guide us into the future. The light of the Guardians will continue to illuminate our path, just as it always has."

AS THE WEEKS TURNED into months, our efforts to uncover the secrets of the ancient ruins continued. The knowledge we gained provided valuable insights into the early teachings of the Guardians and guided our efforts to create a harmonious and just society.

One evening, as the sun set and cast a warm golden light over the village, we gathered in the town square to celebrate the Festival of Unity. The air was filled with the sounds of laughter and music, and the scent of delicious food wafted through the streets. The festival was a time to reflect on our journey, celebrate our achievements, and look forward to the future.

As I stood on the stage, addressing the gathered crowd, I felt a deep sense of pride and gratitude. "Tonight, we celebrate the unity and strength that have brought us here. We have faced darkness and emerged stronger. Our communities are thriving, and the legacy of the Guardians continues to guide us."

The crowd erupted in cheers, their faces filled with joy and hope. The sense of camaraderie and mutual support was palpable, and I could see the strength and resilience of our people shining through.

Daniel, Clara, Lucas, Elara, and Alaric joined me on the stage, their presence a testament to the bonds we had forged and the journey we had undertaken. Together, we looked out at the faces of our friends and allies, our hearts filled with hope and determination.

AS THE FESTIVAL CONTINUED, I found a moment of quiet reflection, standing at the edge of the village and gazing up at the stars. The night was clear, and the constellations seemed to twinkle with a gentle, comforting light. I felt the presence of the Guardians, their wisdom and strength a constant guide.

Daniel joined me, his presence a comforting balm to my soul. "Olivia, you have been our guiding light. Your strength and determination have inspired us all. Together, we will continue to build a future filled with hope and promise."

I smiled, feeling a deep sense of pride and gratitude. "Thank you, Daniel. Our bond has been our greatest strength. Together, we can face anything."

He took my hand, his touch warm and reassuring. "Our journey is far from over, but I know that we can handle whatever comes next. The light of the Guardians will continue to guide us, illuminating the path to a brighter tomorrow."

As we stood together, the gentle light of the stars casting a soothing glow over the village, I made a silent vow. We would continue to protect our world, no matter the cost. With the strength and resilience of our community, and the deepening bond between us, we would face

whatever challenges lay ahead and build a future filled with promise and possibility.

The legacy of the Guardians would continue to shine, guiding us through the darkness and illuminating the path to a brighter tomorrow. And together, we would build a world filled with hope, unity, and endless possibilities.

### **CHAPTER 37: GUARDIANS' Resolve**

The sun continued to shine brightly over Ravenswood, casting a warm glow that infused the village with energy and hope. Our journey to uncover the secrets of the ancient ruins had deepened our understanding of the Guardians' legacy and strengthened our resolve to protect our world. The bonds we had forged were unbreakable, and our community thrived under the guidance of the council of Guardians.

One crisp morning, as the village buzzed with activity and the fields were vibrant with summer growth, Daniel and I met with the council to discuss the progress of our research and the next steps we needed to take. The council chamber was filled with an air of anticipation, and the faces of the council members reflected their dedication and determination.

"Olivia, Daniel," Clara began, her voice steady and authoritative, "our research has uncovered significant insights into the early teachings of the Guardians. We now have a deeper understanding of their commitment to balance, harmony, and wisdom. However, there is still much more to learn. We need to continue our exploration and ensure that we preserve this knowledge for future generations."

Lucas nodded in agreement. "The symbols and inscriptions we've found are invaluable. We must study them carefully and use that knowledge to guide our efforts in the present and future."

Elara, ever the strategist, added, "We should also focus on sharing our discoveries with neighboring communities. The knowledge we've gained can help others strengthen their defenses and protect their worlds."

Alaric, his presence radiating confidence, said, "I'll oversee the preservation efforts and ensure that the ruins remain intact. We cannot afford to make any mistakes."

Daniel, standing beside me, placed a reassuring hand on my shoulder. "We'll face this together, Olivia. Our bond is our strength, and we can overcome any challenge."

I took a deep breath, feeling the weight of the responsibility before us. "Let's do this. We'll continue to uncover the secrets of the past and use that knowledge to build a future filled with hope and promise."

IN THE DAYS THAT FOLLOWED, the village of Ravenswood was a hive of activity. The council of Guardians and our team of researchers worked tirelessly to document and study the symbols and inscriptions found in the ancient ruins. The sense of unity and collaboration was strong, and it filled us with hope for the future.

Clara's expertise in ancient languages and symbols proved invaluable as she continued to translate the inscriptions. "These carvings speak of the early Guardians' commitment to unity and compassion. Their teachings emphasize the importance of working together and supporting one another."

Lucas nodded in agreement. "The artifacts we've found here also suggest that the early Guardians valued both magic and practical knowledge. They sought to use their abilities to protect and nurture their communities."

Elara's strategic mind helped us plan our excavation and preservation efforts. "We need to be thorough and methodical in our approach. Each discovery could provide valuable insights into the history and wisdom of the Guardians."

Alaric's leadership ensured that our efforts were carried out with care and precision. "We'll take every precaution to preserve the integrity of the ruins. This place is a testament to the strength and wisdom of the Guardians, and we must honor and protect it."

AS WE CONTINUED OUR research and exploration, we uncovered more about the history of the Guardians and their early teachings. The sense of connection to the past was profound, and it filled us with a renewed sense of purpose and determination.

One evening, as the sun set and cast a warm golden light over the ancient ruins, Daniel and I found a moment of quiet reflection. We stood in the clearing, gazing at the weathered stones and the intricate carvings that told the story of our ancestors.

"Olivia," Daniel said softly, "this place is a testament to the strength and wisdom of the Guardians. Their legacy continues to guide us, and it's our responsibility to honor and preserve it."

I smiled, feeling a deep sense of pride and gratitude. "Thank you, Daniel. Our bond and our connection to the Guardians have been our greatest strengths. Together, we can continue to protect our world and build a future filled with hope and promise."

He took my hand, his touch warm and reassuring. "We'll continue to uncover the secrets of the past and use that knowledge to guide us into the future. The light of the Guardians will continue to illuminate our path, just as it always has."

AS THE WEEKS TURNED into months, our efforts to uncover the secrets of the ancient ruins continued. The knowledge we gained provided valuable insights into the early teachings of the Guardians and guided our efforts to create a harmonious and just society.

One evening, as the sun set and cast a warm golden light over the village, we gathered in the town square to celebrate the Festival of Unity. The air was filled with the sounds of laughter and music, and the scent of delicious food wafted through the streets. The festival was a time to reflect on our journey, celebrate our achievements, and look forward to the future.

As I stood on the stage, addressing the gathered crowd, I felt a deep sense of pride and gratitude. "Tonight, we celebrate the unity and strength that have brought us here. We have faced darkness and emerged stronger. Our communities are thriving, and the legacy of the Guardians continues to guide us."

The crowd erupted in cheers, their faces filled with joy and hope. The sense of camaraderie and mutual support was palpable, and I could see the strength and resilience of our people shining through.

Daniel, Clara, Lucas, Elara, and Alaric joined me on the stage, their presence a testament to the bonds we had forged and the journey we had undertaken. Together, we looked out at the faces of our friends and allies, our hearts filled with hope and determination.

AS THE FESTIVAL CONTINUED, I found a moment of quiet reflection, standing at the edge of the village and gazing up at the stars. The night was clear, and the constellations seemed to twinkle with a gentle, comforting light. I felt the presence of the Guardians, their wisdom and strength a constant guide.

Daniel joined me, his presence a comforting balm to my soul. "Olivia, you have been our guiding light. Your strength and determination have inspired us all. Together, we will continue to build a future filled with hope and promise."

I smiled, feeling a deep sense of pride and gratitude. "Thank you, Daniel. Our bond has been our greatest strength. Together, we can face anything."

He took my hand, his touch warm and reassuring. "Our journey is far from over, but I know that we can handle whatever comes next. The light of the Guardians will continue to guide us, illuminating the path to a brighter tomorrow."

As we stood together, the gentle light of the stars casting a soothing glow over the village, I made a silent vow. We would continue to protect our world, no matter the cost. With the strength and resilience of our community, and the deepening bond between us, we would face whatever challenges lay ahead and build a future filled with promise and possibility.

The legacy of the Guardians would continue to shine, guiding us through the darkness and illuminating the path to a brighter tomorrow. And together, we would build a world filled with hope, unity, and endless possibilities.

### **CHAPTER 38: THE Light of Discovery**

The warmth of the summer sun continued to bathe Ravenswood in a golden glow, infusing the village with vibrant energy and the promise of new discoveries. Our journey to uncover the secrets of the ancient ruins had deepened our understanding of the Guardians' legacy and strengthened our resolve to protect our world. The unity and strength that had carried us through countless challenges now flourished in the light of the new season.

One bright morning, as the village buzzed with activity and the fields were lush with growth, Daniel and I met with the council to discuss the progress of our research and the exciting discoveries we had made. The council chamber was filled with an air of anticipation, and the faces of the council members reflected their dedication and determination.

"Olivia, Daniel," Clara began, her voice steady and authoritative, "our research has uncovered invaluable insights into the early teachings of the Guardians. We now have a deeper understanding of their commitment to balance, harmony, and wisdom. However, there is still much more to learn. We need to continue our exploration and ensure that we preserve this knowledge for future generations."

Lucas nodded in agreement. "The symbols and inscriptions we've found are a treasure trove of knowledge. We must study them carefully and use that knowledge to guide our efforts in the present and future."

Elara, ever the strategist, added, "We should also focus on sharing our discoveries with neighboring communities. The knowledge we've gained can help others strengthen their defenses and protect their worlds."

Alaric, his presence radiating confidence, said, "I'll oversee the preservation efforts and ensure that the ruins remain intact. We cannot afford to make any mistakes."

Daniel, standing beside me, placed a reassuring hand on my shoulder. "We'll face this together, Olivia. Our bond is our strength, and we can overcome any challenge."

I took a deep breath, feeling the weight of the responsibility before us. "Let's do this. We'll continue to uncover the secrets of the past and use that knowledge to build a future filled with hope and promise."

IN THE DAYS THAT FOLLOWED, the village of Ravenswood was a hive of activity. The council of Guardians and our team of researchers worked tirelessly to document and study the symbols and inscriptions found in the ancient ruins. The sense of unity and collaboration was strong, and it filled us with hope for the future.

Clara's expertise in ancient languages and symbols proved invaluable as she continued to translate the inscriptions. "These carvings speak of the early Guardians' commitment to unity and compassion. Their teachings emphasize the importance of working together and supporting one another."

Lucas nodded in agreement. "The artifacts we've found here also suggest that the early Guardians valued both magic and practical knowledge. They sought to use their abilities to protect and nurture their communities."

Elara's strategic mind helped us plan our excavation and preservation efforts. "We need to be thorough and methodical in our approach. Each discovery could provide valuable insights into the history and wisdom of the Guardians."

Alaric's leadership ensured that our efforts were carried out with care and precision. "We'll take every precaution to preserve the integrity of the ruins. This place is a testament to the strength and wisdom of the Guardians, and we must honor and protect it."

AS WE CONTINUED OUR research and exploration, we uncovered more about the history of the Guardians and their early teachings. The sense of connection to the past was profound, and it filled us with a renewed sense of purpose and determination.

One evening, as the sun set and cast a warm golden light over the ancient ruins, Daniel and I found a moment of quiet reflection. We stood in the clearing, gazing at the weathered stones and the intricate carvings that told the story of our ancestors.

"Olivia," Daniel said softly, "this place is a testament to the strength and wisdom of the Guardians. Their legacy continues to guide us, and it's our responsibility to honor and preserve it."

I smiled, feeling a deep sense of pride and gratitude. "Thank you, Daniel. Our bond and our connection to the Guardians have been our greatest strengths. Together, we can continue to protect our world and build a future filled with hope and promise."

He took my hand, his touch warm and reassuring. "We'll continue to uncover the secrets of the past and use that knowledge to guide us into the future. The light of the Guardians will continue to illuminate our path, just as it always has."

AS THE WEEKS TURNED into months, our efforts to uncover the secrets of the ancient ruins continued. The knowledge we gained provided valuable insights into the early teachings of the Guardians and guided our efforts to create a harmonious and just society.

One evening, as the sun set and cast a warm golden light over the village, we gathered in the town square to celebrate the Festival of Unity. The air was filled with the sounds of laughter and music, and the scent of delicious food wafted through the streets. The festival was a time to reflect on our journey, celebrate our achievements, and look forward to the future.

As I stood on the stage, addressing the gathered crowd, I felt a deep sense of pride and gratitude. "Tonight, we celebrate the unity and strength that have brought us here. We have faced darkness and emerged stronger. Our communities are thriving, and the legacy of the Guardians continues to guide us."

The crowd erupted in cheers, their faces filled with joy and hope. The sense of camaraderie and mutual support was palpable, and I could see the strength and resilience of our people shining through.

Daniel, Clara, Lucas, Elara, and Alaric joined me on the stage, their presence a testament to the bonds we had forged and the journey we had undertaken. Together, we looked out at the faces of our friends and allies, our hearts filled with hope and determination.

AS THE FESTIVAL CONTINUED, I found a moment of quiet reflection, standing at the edge of the village and gazing up at the stars. The night was clear, and the constellations seemed to twinkle with

a gentle, comforting light. I felt the presence of the Guardians, their wisdom and strength a constant guide.

Daniel joined me, his presence a comforting balm to my soul. "Olivia, you have been our guiding light. Your strength and determination have inspired us all. Together, we will continue to build a future filled with hope and promise."

I smiled, feeling a deep sense of pride and gratitude. "Thank you, Daniel. Our bond has been our greatest strength. Together, we can face anything."

He took my hand, his touch warm and reassuring. "Our journey is far from over, but I know that we can handle whatever comes next. The light of the Guardians will continue to guide us, illuminating the path to a brighter tomorrow."

As we stood together, the gentle light of the stars casting a soothing glow over the village, I made a silent vow. We would continue to protect our world, no matter the cost. With the strength and resilience of our community, and the deepening bond between us, we would face whatever challenges lay ahead and build a future filled with promise and possibility.

The legacy of the Guardians would continue to shine, guiding us through the darkness and illuminating the path to a brighter tomorrow. And together, we would build a world filled with hope, unity, and endless possibilities.

### **CHAPTER 39: GUARDIANS' Legacy**

The warm days of summer continued to envelop Ravenswood, filling the village with an air of vitality and promise. The discoveries at the ancient ruins had deepened our understanding of the Guardians' teachings and strengthened our resolve to protect our world. The bonds we had forged were unbreakable, and the legacy of the Guardians continued to guide and inspire us.

One morning, as the village buzzed with activity and the fields thrived with growth, Daniel and I met with the council to discuss our progress and the exciting future that lay ahead. The council chamber was filled with an air of anticipation, and the faces of the council members reflected their dedication and determination.

"Olivia, Daniel," Clara began, her voice steady and authoritative, "our research has provided us with invaluable insights into the early teachings of the Guardians. We now have a deeper understanding of their commitment to balance, harmony, and wisdom. However, there is still much more to learn. We need to continue our exploration and ensure that we preserve this knowledge for future generations."

Lucas nodded in agreement. "The symbols and inscriptions we've found are a treasure trove of knowledge. We must study them carefully and use that knowledge to guide our efforts in the present and future."

Elara, ever the strategist, added, "We should also focus on sharing our discoveries with neighboring communities. The knowledge we've gained can help others strengthen their defenses and protect their worlds."

Alaric, his presence radiating confidence, said, "I'll oversee the preservation efforts and ensure that the ruins remain intact. We cannot afford to make any mistakes."

Daniel, standing beside me, placed a reassuring hand on my shoulder. "We'll face this together, Olivia. Our bond is our strength, and we can overcome any challenge."

I took a deep breath, feeling the weight of the responsibility before us. "Let's do this. We'll continue to uncover the secrets of the past and use that knowledge to build a future filled with hope and promise."

IN THE DAYS THAT FOLLOWED, the village of Ravenswood was a hive of activity. The council of Guardians and our team of researchers worked tirelessly to document and study the symbols and inscriptions found in the ancient ruins. The sense of unity and collaboration was strong, and it filled us with hope for the future.

Clara's expertise in ancient languages and symbols proved invaluable as she continued to translate the inscriptions. "These carvings speak of the early Guardians' commitment to unity and compassion. Their teachings emphasize the importance of working together and supporting one another."

Lucas nodded in agreement. "The artifacts we've found here also suggest that the early Guardians valued both magic and practical knowledge. They sought to use their abilities to protect and nurture their communities."

Elara's strategic mind helped us plan our excavation and preservation efforts. "We need to be thorough and methodical in our approach. Each discovery could provide valuable insights into the history and wisdom of the Guardians."

Alaric's leadership ensured that our efforts were carried out with care and precision. "We'll take every precaution to preserve the integrity of the ruins. This place is a testament to the strength and wisdom of the Guardians, and we must honor and protect it."

AS WE CONTINUED OUR research and exploration, we uncovered more about the history of the Guardians and their early teachings. The sense of connection to the past was profound, and it filled us with a renewed sense of purpose and determination.

One evening, as the sun set and cast a warm golden light over the ancient ruins, Daniel and I found a moment of quiet reflection. We stood in the clearing, gazing at the weathered stones and the intricate carvings that told the story of our ancestors.

"Olivia," Daniel said softly, "this place is a testament to the strength and wisdom of the Guardians. Their legacy continues to guide us, and it's our responsibility to honor and preserve it."

I smiled, feeling a deep sense of pride and gratitude. "Thank you, Daniel. Our bond and our connection to the Guardians have been our greatest strengths. Together, we can continue to protect our world and build a future filled with hope and promise."

He took my hand, his touch warm and reassuring. "We'll continue to uncover the secrets of the past and use that knowledge to guide us into the future. The light of the Guardians will continue to illuminate our path, just as it always has."

AS THE WEEKS TURNED into months, our efforts to uncover the secrets of the ancient ruins continued. The knowledge we gained provided valuable insights into the early teachings of the Guardians and guided our efforts to create a harmonious and just society.

One evening, as the sun set and cast a warm golden light over the village, we gathered in the town square to celebrate the Festival of Unity. The air was filled with the sounds of laughter and music, and the scent of delicious food wafted through the streets. The festival was a time to reflect on our journey, celebrate our achievements, and look forward to the future.

As I stood on the stage, addressing the gathered crowd, I felt a deep sense of pride and gratitude. "Tonight, we celebrate the unity and strength that have brought us here. We have faced darkness and emerged stronger. Our communities are thriving, and the legacy of the Guardians continues to guide us."

The crowd erupted in cheers, their faces filled with joy and hope. The sense of camaraderie and mutual support was palpable, and I could see the strength and resilience of our people shining through.

Daniel, Clara, Lucas, Elara, and Alaric joined me on the stage, their presence a testament to the bonds we had forged and the journey we had undertaken. Together, we looked out at the faces of our friends and allies, our hearts filled with hope and determination.

AS THE FESTIVAL CONTINUED, I found a moment of quiet reflection, standing at the edge of the village and gazing up at the stars. The night was clear, and the constellations seemed to twinkle with a gentle, comforting light. I felt the presence of the Guardians, their wisdom and strength a constant guide.

Daniel joined me, his presence a comforting balm to my soul. "Olivia, you have been our guiding light. Your strength and determination have inspired us all. Together, we will continue to build a future filled with hope and promise."

I smiled, feeling a deep sense of pride and gratitude. "Thank you, Daniel. Our bond has been our greatest strength. Together, we can face anything."

He took my hand, his touch warm and reassuring. "Our journey is far from over, but I know that we can handle whatever comes next. The light of the Guardians will continue to guide us, illuminating the path to a brighter tomorrow."

As we stood together, the gentle light of the stars casting a soothing glow over the village, I made a silent vow. We would continue to protect our world, no matter the cost. With the strength and resilience of our community, and the deepening bond between us, we would face whatever challenges lay ahead and build a future filled with promise and possibility.

The legacy of the Guardians would continue to shine, guiding us through the darkness and illuminating the path to a brighter tomorrow. And together, we would build a world filled with hope, unity, and endless possibilities.

### **CHAPTER 40: GUARDIANS' Promise**

The golden hues of late summer cast a warm glow over Ravenswood, filling the village with an aura of vitality and the promise of new beginnings. Our exploration of the ancient ruins had yielded invaluable insights into the teachings of the Guardians, deepening our connection to their legacy and strengthening our resolve to protect our world. The bonds we had forged were unbreakable, and the unity and strength of our community continued to thrive.

One morning, as the village buzzed with activity and the fields flourished with growth, Daniel and I met with the council to discuss our progress and the exciting future that lay ahead. The council chamber was filled with an air of anticipation, and the faces of the council members reflected their dedication and determination.

"Olivia, Daniel," Clara began, her voice steady and authoritative, "our research has provided us with invaluable insights into the early teachings of the Guardians. We now have a deeper understanding of their commitment to balance, harmony, and wisdom. However, there is still much more to learn. We need to continue our exploration and ensure that we preserve this knowledge for future generations."

Lucas nodded in agreement. "The symbols and inscriptions we've found are a treasure trove of knowledge. We must study them carefully and use that knowledge to guide our efforts in the present and future."

Elara, ever the strategist, added, "We should also focus on sharing our discoveries with neighboring communities. The knowledge we've gained can help others strengthen their defenses and protect their worlds."

Alaric, his presence radiating confidence, said, "I'll oversee the preservation efforts and ensure that the ruins remain intact. We cannot afford to make any mistakes."

Daniel, standing beside me, placed a reassuring hand on my shoulder. "We'll face this together, Olivia. Our bond is our strength, and we can overcome any challenge."

I took a deep breath, feeling the weight of the responsibility before us. "Let's do this. We'll continue to uncover the secrets of the past and use that knowledge to build a future filled with hope and promise."

IN THE DAYS THAT FOLLOWED, the village of Ravenswood was a hive of activity. The council of Guardians and our team of researchers worked tirelessly to document and study the symbols and inscriptions found in the ancient ruins. The sense of unity and collaboration was strong, and it filled us with hope for the future.

Clara's expertise in ancient languages and symbols proved invaluable as she continued to translate the inscriptions. "These carvings speak of the early Guardians' commitment to unity and compassion. Their teachings emphasize the importance of working together and supporting one another."

Lucas nodded in agreement. "The artifacts we've found here also suggest that the early Guardians valued both magic and practical knowledge. They sought to use their abilities to protect and nurture their communities."

Elara's strategic mind helped us plan our excavation and preservation efforts. "We need to be thorough and methodical in our approach. Each discovery could provide valuable insights into the history and wisdom of the Guardians."

Alaric's leadership ensured that our efforts were carried out with care and precision. "We'll take every precaution to preserve the integrity of the ruins. This place is a testament to the strength and wisdom of the Guardians, and we must honor and protect it."

AS WE CONTINUED OUR research and exploration, we uncovered more about the history of the Guardians and their early teachings. The sense of connection to the past was profound, and it filled us with a renewed sense of purpose and determination.

One evening, as the sun set and cast a warm golden light over the ancient ruins, Daniel and I found a moment of quiet reflection. We stood in the clearing, gazing at the weathered stones and the intricate carvings that told the story of our ancestors.

"Olivia," Daniel said softly, "this place is a testament to the strength and wisdom of the Guardians. Their legacy continues to guide us, and it's our responsibility to honor and preserve it."

I smiled, feeling a deep sense of pride and gratitude. "Thank you, Daniel. Our bond and our connection to the Guardians have been our greatest strengths. Together, we can continue to protect our world and build a future filled with hope and promise."

He took my hand, his touch warm and reassuring. "We'll continue to uncover the secrets of the past and use that knowledge to guide us into the future. The light of the Guardians will continue to illuminate our path, just as it always has."

AS THE WEEKS TURNED into months, our efforts to uncover the secrets of the ancient ruins continued. The knowledge we gained provided valuable insights into the early teachings of the Guardians and guided our efforts to create a harmonious and just society.

One evening, as the sun set and cast a warm golden light over the village, we gathered in the town square to celebrate the Festival of Unity. The air was filled with the sounds of laughter and music, and the scent of delicious food wafted through the streets. The festival was a time to reflect on our journey, celebrate our achievements, and look forward to the future.

As I stood on the stage, addressing the gathered crowd, I felt a deep sense of pride and gratitude. "Tonight, we celebrate the unity and strength that have brought us here. We have faced darkness and emerged stronger. Our communities are thriving, and the legacy of the Guardians continues to guide us."

The crowd erupted in cheers, their faces filled with joy and hope. The sense of camaraderie and mutual support was palpable, and I could see the strength and resilience of our people shining through.

Daniel, Clara, Lucas, Elara, and Alaric joined me on the stage, their presence a testament to the bonds we had forged and the journey we had undertaken. Together, we looked out at the faces of our friends and allies, our hearts filled with hope and determination.

AS THE FESTIVAL CONTINUED, I found a moment of quiet reflection, standing at the edge of the village and gazing up at the stars. The night was clear, and the constellations seemed to twinkle with a gentle, comforting light. I felt the presence of the Guardians, their wisdom and strength a constant guide.

Daniel joined me, his presence a comforting balm to my soul. "Olivia, you have been our guiding light. Your strength and determination have inspired us all. Together, we will continue to build a future filled with hope and promise."

I smiled, feeling a deep sense of pride and gratitude. "Thank you, Daniel. Our bond has been our greatest strength. Together, we can face anything."

He took my hand, his touch warm and reassuring. "Our journey is far from over, but I know that we can handle whatever comes next. The light of the Guardians will continue to guide us, illuminating the path to a brighter tomorrow."

As we stood together, the gentle light of the stars casting a soothing glow over the village, I made a silent vow. We would continue to protect our world, no matter the cost. With the strength and resilience of our community, and the deepening bond between us, we would face

whatever challenges lay ahead and build a future filled with promise and possibility.

The legacy of the Guardians would continue to shine, guiding us through the darkness and illuminating the path to a brighter tomorrow. And together, we would build a world filled with hope, unity, and endless possibilities.

### **CHAPTER 41: A GLIMPSE into Tomorrow**

As the Festival of Unity drew to a close, the village of Ravenswood was filled with a renewed sense of purpose and hope. Our journey to uncover the secrets of the ancient ruins had strengthened our resolve and deepened our connection to the legacy of the Guardians. The unity and strength of our community had never been stronger, and we were determined to protect our world and build a brighter future.

One morning, as the village buzzed with activity and the fields thrived with growth, Daniel and I met with the council to discuss our progress and the exciting opportunities that lay ahead. The council chamber was filled with an air of anticipation, and the faces of the council members reflected their dedication and determination.

"Olivia, Daniel," Clara began, her voice steady and authoritative, "our research has provided us with invaluable insights into the early teachings of the Guardians. We now have a deeper understanding of their commitment to balance, harmony, and wisdom. However, there is still much more to learn. We need to continue our exploration and ensure that we preserve this knowledge for future generations."

Lucas nodded in agreement. "The symbols and inscriptions we've found are a treasure trove of knowledge. We must study them carefully and use that knowledge to guide our efforts in the present and future."

Elara, ever the strategist, added, "We should also focus on sharing our discoveries with neighboring communities. The knowledge we've gained can help others strengthen their defenses and protect their worlds."

Alaric, his presence radiating confidence, said, "I'll oversee the preservation efforts and ensure that the ruins remain intact. We cannot afford to make any mistakes."

Daniel, standing beside me, placed a reassuring hand on my shoulder. "We'll face this together, Olivia. Our bond is our strength, and we can overcome any challenge."

I took a deep breath, feeling the weight of the responsibility before us. "Let's do this. We'll continue to uncover the secrets of the past and use that knowledge to build a future filled with hope and promise."

IN THE DAYS THAT FOLLOWED, the village of Ravenswood was a hive of activity. The council of Guardians and our team of researchers worked tirelessly to document and study the symbols and inscriptions found in the ancient ruins. The sense of unity and collaboration was strong, and it filled us with hope for the future.

Clara's expertise in ancient languages and symbols proved invaluable as she continued to translate the inscriptions. "These carvings speak of the early Guardians' commitment to unity and compassion. Their teachings emphasize the importance of working together and supporting one another."

Lucas nodded in agreement. "The artifacts we've found here also suggest that the early Guardians valued both magic and practical knowledge. They sought to use their abilities to protect and nurture their communities."

Elara's strategic mind helped us plan our excavation and preservation efforts. "We need to be thorough and methodical in our approach. Each discovery could provide valuable insights into the history and wisdom of the Guardians."

Alaric's leadership ensured that our efforts were carried out with care and precision. "We'll take every precaution to preserve the integrity of the ruins. This place is a testament to the strength and wisdom of the Guardians, and we must honor and protect it."

AS WE CONTINUED OUR research and exploration, we uncovered more about the history of the Guardians and their early teachings. The sense of connection to the past was profound, and it filled us with a renewed sense of purpose and determination.

One evening, as the sun set and cast a warm golden light over the ancient ruins, Daniel and I found a moment of quiet reflection. We stood in the clearing, gazing at the weathered stones and the intricate carvings that told the story of our ancestors.

"Olivia," Daniel said softly, "this place is a testament to the strength and wisdom of the Guardians. Their legacy continues to guide us, and it's our responsibility to honor and preserve it."

I smiled, feeling a deep sense of pride and gratitude. "Thank you, Daniel. Our bond and our connection to the Guardians have been our greatest strengths. Together, we can continue to protect our world and build a future filled with hope and promise."

He took my hand, his touch warm and reassuring. "We'll continue to uncover the secrets of the past and use that knowledge to guide us into the future. The light of the Guardians will continue to illuminate our path, just as it always has."

AS THE WEEKS TURNED into months, our efforts to uncover the secrets of the ancient ruins continued. The knowledge we gained provided valuable insights into the early teachings of the Guardians and guided our efforts to create a harmonious and just society.

One evening, as the sun set and cast a warm golden light over the village, we gathered in the town square to celebrate the Festival of Unity. The air was filled with the sounds of laughter and music, and the scent of delicious food wafted through the streets. The festival was a time to reflect on our journey, celebrate our achievements, and look forward to the future.

As I stood on the stage, addressing the gathered crowd, I felt a deep sense of pride and gratitude. "Tonight, we celebrate the unity and strength that have brought us here. We have faced darkness and emerged stronger. Our communities are thriving, and the legacy of the Guardians continues to guide us."

The crowd erupted in cheers, their faces filled with joy and hope. The sense of camaraderie and mutual support was palpable, and I could see the strength and resilience of our people shining through.

Daniel, Clara, Lucas, Elara, and Alaric joined me on the stage, their presence a testament to the bonds we had forged and the journey we had undertaken. Together, we looked out at the faces of our friends and allies, our hearts filled with hope and determination.

AS THE FESTIVAL CONTINUED, I found a moment of quiet reflection, standing at the edge of the village and gazing up at the stars. The night was clear, and the constellations seemed to twinkle with a gentle, comforting light. I felt the presence of the Guardians, their wisdom and strength a constant guide.

Daniel joined me, his presence a comforting balm to my soul. "Olivia, you have been our guiding light. Your strength and determination have inspired us all. Together, we will continue to build a future filled with hope and promise."

I smiled, feeling a deep sense of pride and gratitude. "Thank you, Daniel. Our bond has been our greatest strength. Together, we can face anything."

He took my hand, his touch warm and reassuring. "Our journey is far from over, but I know that we can handle whatever comes next. The light of the Guardians will continue to guide us, illuminating the path to a brighter tomorrow."

As we stood together, the gentle light of the stars casting a soothing glow over the village, I made a silent vow. We would continue to protect our world, no matter the cost. With the strength and resilience of our community, and the deepening bond between us, we would face whatever challenges lay ahead and build a future filled with promise and possibility.

The legacy of the Guardians would continue to shine, guiding us through the darkness and illuminating the path to a brighter tomorrow. And together, we would build a world filled with hope, unity, and endless possibilities.

### **CHAPTER 42: GUARDIANS' Path**

The warmth of the late summer sun continued to bathe Ravenswood in golden light, imbuing the village with a sense of vitality and optimism. Our efforts to uncover the secrets of the ancient ruins had deepened our connection to the Guardians and their teachings, strengthening our resolve to protect our world. The bonds we had forged were unbreakable, and the unity and strength of our community continued to thrive.

One morning, as the village buzzed with activity and the fields flourished, Daniel and I gathered with the council to discuss our progress and the exciting future that lay ahead. The council chamber was filled with an air of anticipation, and the faces of the council members reflected their dedication and determination.

"Olivia, Daniel," Clara began, her voice steady and authoritative, "our research has provided us with invaluable insights into the early teachings of the Guardians. We now have a deeper understanding of their commitment to balance, harmony, and wisdom. However, there is still much more to learn. We need to continue our exploration and ensure that we preserve this knowledge for future generations."

Lucas nodded in agreement. "The symbols and inscriptions we've found are a treasure trove of knowledge. We must study them carefully and use that knowledge to guide our efforts in the present and future."

Elara, ever the strategist, added, "We should also focus on sharing our discoveries with neighboring communities. The knowledge we've gained can help others strengthen their defenses and protect their worlds."

Alaric, his presence radiating confidence, said, "I'll oversee the preservation efforts and ensure that the ruins remain intact. We cannot afford to make any mistakes."

Daniel, standing beside me, placed a reassuring hand on my shoulder. "We'll face this together, Olivia. Our bond is our strength, and we can overcome any challenge."

I took a deep breath, feeling the weight of the responsibility before us. "Let's do this. We'll continue to uncover the secrets of the past and use that knowledge to build a future filled with hope and promise."

IN THE DAYS THAT FOLLOWED, the village of Ravenswood was a hive of activity. The council of Guardians and our team of researchers worked tirelessly to document and study the symbols and inscriptions found in the ancient ruins. The sense of unity and collaboration was strong, and it filled us with hope for the future.

Clara's expertise in ancient languages and symbols proved invaluable as she continued to translate the inscriptions. "These carvings speak of the early Guardians' commitment to unity and compassion. Their teachings emphasize the importance of working together and supporting one another."

Lucas nodded in agreement. "The artifacts we've found here also suggest that the early Guardians valued both magic and practical knowledge. They sought to use their abilities to protect and nurture their communities."

Elara's strategic mind helped us plan our excavation and preservation efforts. "We need to be thorough and methodical in our approach. Each discovery could provide valuable insights into the history and wisdom of the Guardians."

Alaric's leadership ensured that our efforts were carried out with care and precision. "We'll take every precaution to preserve the integrity of the ruins. This place is a testament to the strength and wisdom of the Guardians, and we must honor and protect it."

AS WE CONTINUED OUR research and exploration, we uncovered more about the history of the Guardians and their early teachings. The sense of connection to the past was profound, and it filled us with a renewed sense of purpose and determination.

One evening, as the sun set and cast a warm golden light over the ancient ruins, Daniel and I found a moment of quiet reflection. We stood in the clearing, gazing at the weathered stones and the intricate carvings that told the story of our ancestors.

"Olivia," Daniel said softly, "this place is a testament to the strength and wisdom of the Guardians. Their legacy continues to guide us, and it's our responsibility to honor and preserve it."

I smiled, feeling a deep sense of pride and gratitude. "Thank you, Daniel. Our bond and our connection to the Guardians have been our greatest strengths. Together, we can continue to protect our world and build a future filled with hope and promise."

He took my hand, his touch warm and reassuring. "We'll continue to uncover the secrets of the past and use that knowledge to guide us into the future. The light of the Guardians will continue to illuminate our path, just as it always has."

AS THE WEEKS TURNED into months, our efforts to uncover the secrets of the ancient ruins continued. The knowledge we gained provided valuable insights into the early teachings of the Guardians and guided our efforts to create a harmonious and just society.

One evening, as the sun set and cast a warm golden light over the village, we gathered in the town square to celebrate the Festival of Unity. The air was filled with the sounds of laughter and music, and the scent of delicious food wafted through the streets. The festival was a time to reflect on our journey, celebrate our achievements, and look forward to the future.

As I stood on the stage, addressing the gathered crowd, I felt a deep sense of pride and gratitude. "Tonight, we celebrate the unity and strength that have brought us here. We have faced darkness and emerged stronger. Our communities are thriving, and the legacy of the Guardians continues to guide us."

The crowd erupted in cheers, their faces filled with joy and hope. The sense of camaraderie and mutual support was palpable, and I could see the strength and resilience of our people shining through.

Daniel, Clara, Lucas, Elara, and Alaric joined me on the stage, their presence a testament to the bonds we had forged and the journey we had undertaken. Together, we looked out at the faces of our friends and allies, our hearts filled with hope and determination.

AS THE FESTIVAL CONTINUED, I found a moment of quiet reflection, standing at the edge of the village and gazing up at the stars. The night was clear, and the constellations seemed to twinkle with

a gentle, comforting light. I felt the presence of the Guardians, their wisdom and strength a constant guide.

Daniel joined me, his presence a comforting balm to my soul. "Olivia, you have been our guiding light. Your strength and determination have inspired us all. Together, we will continue to build a future filled with hope and promise."

I smiled, feeling a deep sense of pride and gratitude. "Thank you, Daniel. Our bond has been our greatest strength. Together, we can face anything."

He took my hand, his touch warm and reassuring. "Our journey is far from over, but I know that we can handle whatever comes next. The light of the Guardians will continue to guide us, illuminating the path to a brighter tomorrow."

As we stood together, the gentle light of the stars casting a soothing glow over the village, I made a silent vow. We would continue to protect our world, no matter the cost. With the strength and resilience of our community, and the deepening bond between us, we would face whatever challenges lay ahead and build a future filled with promise and possibility.

The legacy of the Guardians would continue to shine, guiding us through the darkness and illuminating the path to a brighter tomorrow. And together, we would build a world filled with hope, unity, and endless possibilities.

### **CHAPTER 43: GUARDIANS' Wisdom**

The transition from summer to autumn brought a kaleidoscope of colors to Ravenswood. The trees adorned themselves in vibrant hues of red, gold, and orange, and the crisp air carried the promise of new discoveries. Our efforts to uncover the secrets of the ancient ruins had deepened our connection to the Guardians and their teachings, strengthening our resolve to protect our world. The unity and strength of our community continued to thrive, and the bonds we had forged were unbreakable.

One morning, as the village buzzed with activity and the fields were ripe with harvest, Daniel and I gathered with the council to discuss our progress and the exciting future that lay ahead. The council chamber was filled with an air of anticipation, and the faces of the council members reflected their dedication and determination.

"Olivia, Daniel," Clara began, her voice steady and authoritative, "our research has provided us with invaluable insights into the early teachings of the Guardians. We now have a deeper understanding of their commitment to balance, harmony, and wisdom. However, there is still much more to learn. We need to continue our exploration and ensure that we preserve this knowledge for future generations."

Lucas nodded in agreement. "The symbols and inscriptions we've found are a treasure trove of knowledge. We must study them carefully and use that knowledge to guide our efforts in the present and future."

Elara, ever the strategist, added, "We should also focus on sharing our discoveries with neighboring communities. The knowledge we've gained can help others strengthen their defenses and protect their worlds."

Alaric, his presence radiating confidence, said, "I'll oversee the preservation efforts and ensure that the ruins remain intact. We cannot afford to make any mistakes."

Daniel, standing beside me, placed a reassuring hand on my shoulder. "We'll face this together, Olivia. Our bond is our strength, and we can overcome any challenge."

I took a deep breath, feeling the weight of the responsibility before us. "Let's do this. We'll continue to uncover the secrets of the past and use that knowledge to build a future filled with hope and promise."

IN THE DAYS THAT FOLLOWED, the village of Ravenswood was a hive of activity. The council of Guardians and our team of researchers worked tirelessly to document and study the symbols and inscriptions found in the ancient ruins. The sense of unity and collaboration was strong, and it filled us with hope for the future.

Clara's expertise in ancient languages and symbols proved invaluable as she continued to translate the inscriptions. "These carvings speak of the early Guardians' commitment to unity and compassion. Their teachings emphasize the importance of working together and supporting one another."

Lucas nodded in agreement. "The artifacts we've found here also suggest that the early Guardians valued both magic and practical knowledge. They sought to use their abilities to protect and nurture their communities."

Elara's strategic mind helped us plan our excavation and preservation efforts. "We need to be thorough and methodical in our approach. Each discovery could provide valuable insights into the history and wisdom of the Guardians."

Alaric's leadership ensured that our efforts were carried out with care and precision. "We'll take every precaution to preserve the integrity of the ruins. This place is a testament to the strength and wisdom of the Guardians, and we must honor and protect it."

AS WE CONTINUED OUR research and exploration, we uncovered more about the history of the Guardians and their early teachings. The sense of connection to the past was profound, and it filled us with a renewed sense of purpose and determination.

One evening, as the sun set and cast a warm golden light over the ancient ruins, Daniel and I found a moment of quiet reflection. We stood in the clearing, gazing at the weathered stones and the intricate carvings that told the story of our ancestors.

"Olivia," Daniel said softly, "this place is a testament to the strength and wisdom of the Guardians. Their legacy continues to guide us, and it's our responsibility to honor and preserve it."

I smiled, feeling a deep sense of pride and gratitude. "Thank you, Daniel. Our bond and our connection to the Guardians have been our greatest strengths. Together, we can continue to protect our world and build a future filled with hope and promise."

He took my hand, his touch warm and reassuring. "We'll continue to uncover the secrets of the past and use that knowledge to guide us into the future. The light of the Guardians will continue to illuminate our path, just as it always has."

AS THE WEEKS TURNED into months, our efforts to uncover the secrets of the ancient ruins continued. The knowledge we gained provided valuable insights into the early teachings of the Guardians and guided our efforts to create a harmonious and just society.

One evening, as the sun set and cast a warm golden light over the village, we gathered in the town square to celebrate the Festival of Wisdom. The air was filled with the sounds of laughter and music, and the scent of delicious food wafted through the streets. The festival was a time to reflect on our journey, celebrate our achievements, and look forward to the future.

As I stood on the stage, addressing the gathered crowd, I felt a deep sense of pride and gratitude. "Tonight, we celebrate the wisdom and knowledge that have brought us here. We have faced darkness and emerged stronger. Our communities are thriving, and the legacy of the Guardians continues to guide us."

The crowd erupted in cheers, their faces filled with joy and hope. The sense of camaraderie and mutual support was palpable, and I could see the strength and resilience of our people shining through.

Daniel, Clara, Lucas, Elara, and Alaric joined me on the stage, their presence a testament to the bonds we had forged and the journey we had undertaken. Together, we looked out at the faces of our friends and allies, our hearts filled with hope and determination.

AS THE FESTIVAL CONTINUED, I found a moment of quiet reflection, standing at the edge of the village and gazing up at the stars. The night was clear, and the constellations seemed to twinkle with a gentle, comforting light. I felt the presence of the Guardians, their wisdom and strength a constant guide.

Daniel joined me, his presence a comforting balm to my soul. "Olivia, you have been our guiding light. Your strength and determination have inspired us all. Together, we will continue to build a future filled with hope and promise."

I smiled, feeling a deep sense of pride and gratitude. "Thank you, Daniel. Our bond has been our greatest strength. Together, we can face anything."

He took my hand, his touch warm and reassuring. "Our journey is far from over, but I know that we can handle whatever comes next. The light of the Guardians will continue to guide us, illuminating the path to a brighter tomorrow."

As we stood together, the gentle light of the stars casting a soothing glow over the village, I made a silent vow. We would continue to protect our world, no matter the cost. With the strength and resilience of our community, and the deepening bond between us, we would face whatever challenges lay ahead and build a future filled with promise and possibility.

The legacy of the Guardians would continue to shine, guiding us through the darkness and illuminating the path to a brighter tomorrow. And together, we would build a world filled with hope, unity, and endless possibilities.

### **CHAPTER 44: PLANNING for Forever**

The village of Ravenswood was aglow with the vibrant colors of autumn, and a sense of joy and anticipation filled the air. The discoveries at the ancient ruins had deepened our connection to the Guardians and strengthened our resolve to protect our world. As the leaves turned shades of gold and crimson, Daniel and I found ourselves looking ahead to our future with excitement and love. It was time to plan our wedding.

One crisp morning, as the sunlight filtered through the trees and cast a warm glow over the village, Daniel and I sat down together in our cozy cottage to begin planning our special day. The air was filled with the scent of freshly brewed tea and the promise of new beginnings.

"Olivia," Daniel began, his eyes shining with warmth and affection, "I want our wedding to be a celebration of our love and the journey we've taken together. It should reflect the unity and strength of our community and the legacy of the Guardians."

I smiled, feeling a sense of excitement and joy. "I couldn't agree more, Daniel. Let's make this day truly special, not just for us, but for everyone who has supported us along the way."

We began by discussing the guest list, ensuring that our closest friends, family, and allies would be there to share in our happiness. Clara, Lucas, Elara, and Alaric were at the top of the list, along with many others who had stood by us through thick and thin.

Next, we turned our attention to the venue. We wanted a location that was both meaningful and beautiful, a place that would symbolize our love and the strength of our community.

"How about the clearing by the ancient ruins?" Daniel suggested. "It's where we made so many of our discoveries and deepened our connection to the Guardians. It feels like the perfect place to start our new journey together."

I nodded, feeling a deep sense of connection to the location. "I love that idea, Daniel. The ruins have become a symbol of our past, present, and future. It will be a beautiful and meaningful setting for our wedding."

With the venue decided, we began to think about the details of the ceremony. We wanted it to be a blend of tradition and personal touches, reflecting both our individual personalities and the unity of our bond.

Clara, with her keen sense of organization, offered to help with the planning. "I'll take care of the logistics and make sure everything runs smoothly. From the seating arrangements to the decorations, I've got it covered."

Lucas, ever the scholar, suggested incorporating some of the ancient symbols and inscriptions we had discovered at the ruins into our vows and decorations. "These symbols carry the wisdom and teachings of the Guardians. Including them in your wedding will add a deeper layer of meaning and connection."

Elara, with her strategic mind, helped us plan the layout and flow of the ceremony. "We'll set up the seating in a semicircle around the clearing, facing the ruins. This way, everyone will have a clear view and feel included in the celebration."

Alaric, ever the protector, volunteered to oversee security and ensure that the event remained safe and peaceful. "I'll make sure everything is secure so you can focus on enjoying your special day."

As we continued to plan, the sense of excitement and joy grew. We chose flowers, music, and readings that held special significance for us. Each decision was made with love and care, reflecting our journey and the unity of our bond.

One evening, as the sun set and cast a warm golden light over the village, Daniel and I took a walk through the fields, hand in hand. The sky was a canvas of vibrant colors, and the air was filled with the sweet scent of autumn.

"Olivia," Daniel said softly, "this journey we've taken together has been incredible. I can't wait to spend the rest of my life with you. Our wedding will be the beginning of a new chapter filled with hope and promise."

I smiled, feeling a deep sense of love and gratitude. "Thank you, Daniel. Our bond has been our greatest strength. Together, we can face anything and build a future filled with endless possibilities."

As we stood together, the gentle light of the stars casting a soothing glow over the village, I made a silent vow. We would continue to protect our world, no matter the cost. With the strength and resilience of our community, and the deepening bond between us, we would face whatever challenges lay ahead and build a future filled with promise and possibility.

The legacy of the Guardians would continue to shine, guiding us through the darkness and illuminating the path to a brighter tomorrow. And together, we would build a world filled with hope, unity, and endless possibilities.

### **CHAPTER 45: THE Day of Union**

The days leading up to our wedding were filled with excitement and anticipation. The village of Ravenswood was abuzz with preparations, and the sense of unity and joy was palpable. Friends and family from near and far arrived to join us in celebrating our special day. The air was filled with the scent of blooming flowers and the promise of new beginnings.

One bright morning, as the sunlight filtered through the trees and cast a warm glow over the village, Daniel and I walked to the clearing by the ancient ruins, where our wedding would take place. The site was already being transformed into a beautiful venue, with flowers and decorations adorning the weathered stones and lush greenery.

"Olivia," Daniel said, his eyes shining with love and excitement, "this place is perfect. It's a reflection of our journey and the bond we've forged. I can't wait to start this new chapter with you."

I smiled, feeling a deep sense of happiness and gratitude. "Thank you, Daniel. Our bond has been our greatest strength, and this day will be a celebration of our love and the unity of our community."

THE DAY OF OUR WEDDING arrived, and the village of Ravenswood was transformed into a festive wonderland. The air was filled with the sounds of laughter and music, and the scent of delicious food wafted through the streets. The clearing by the ancient ruins was a vision of beauty, with flowers, lanterns, and intricate decorations that reflected the wisdom and teachings of the Guardians.

As I prepared for the ceremony, surrounded by Clara, Elara, and my closest friends, I felt a sense of calm and contentment wash over me. The love and support of my community were a constant source of strength, and I knew that I was about to embark on a new journey filled with hope and promise.

Clara smiled warmly as she helped me with the final touches of my dress. "Olivia, you look absolutely stunning. This is your day, and it's going to be perfect."

Elara nodded in agreement. "Everything is ready. The decorations, the food, the music—everything reflects the joy and love that you and Daniel share. This is a celebration of your love and the unity of our community."

I took a deep breath, feeling a surge of excitement and anticipation. "Thank you both. Your support means the world to me. I couldn't have asked for better friends."

THE CEREMONY TOOK PLACE in the clearing, surrounded by the beauty of nature and the love of our friends and family. The air was filled with the sounds of music and laughter, and the sense of unity and celebration was palpable.

As I walked down the aisle, my heart swelled with love and joy. Daniel stood at the altar, his eyes filled with warmth and affection. The sight of him waiting for me filled me with a sense of peace and certainty, and I knew that we were meant to be together.

The ceremony was a beautiful reflection of our journey and the bonds we had forged. Clara and Lucas spoke words of love and unity, while Elara and Alaric offered their blessings and support. The sense of joy and celebration was overwhelming, and I couldn't help but feel a deep sense of gratitude for the love and support of our community.

When it was time for our vows, Daniel took my hands in his, his touch warm and reassuring. "Olivia, you are my guiding light. Your strength, determination, and compassion have inspired me every day. I promise to stand by your side, to love and support you, and to face every challenge together."

Tears welled up in my eyes as I spoke my vows. "Daniel, you are my rock, my partner, and my best friend. Your love and support have been a constant source of strength. I promise to stand by your side, to love and support you, and to face every challenge together."

As we exchanged rings and sealed our vows with a kiss, the village erupted in cheers and applause. The sense of unity and celebration was palpable, and I felt a deep sense of joy and contentment.

THE RECEPTION THAT followed was a joyous celebration of love and unity. The air was filled with the sounds of laughter and music, and the village square was alive with dancing and merriment. Friends and family gathered to share in our happiness, and the sense of camaraderie and mutual support was overwhelming.

As the evening progressed, Daniel and I took a moment to step away from the festivities and find a quiet spot at the edge of the village. The night was clear, and the stars twinkled brightly in the sky, casting a gentle, comforting light.

"Olivia," Daniel said softly, "today has been the most beautiful day of my life. Our journey is far from over, but I know that together, we can handle whatever comes next. The light of the Guardians will continue to guide us, illuminating the path to a brighter tomorrow."

I smiled, feeling a deep sense of pride and gratitude. "Thank you, Daniel. Our bond has been our greatest strength. Together, we can face anything."

He took my hand, his touch warm and reassuring. "We'll continue to build a future filled with hope and promise. Our love will guide us through whatever challenges lie ahead."

As we stood together, the gentle light of the stars casting a soothing glow over the village, I made a silent vow. We would continue to protect our world, no matter the cost. With the strength and resilience of our community, and the deepening bond between us, we would face whatever challenges lay ahead and build a future filled with promise and possibility.

The legacy of the Guardians would continue to shine, guiding us through the darkness and illuminating the path to a brighter tomorrow. And together, we would build a world filled with hope, unity, and endless possibilities.

### **CHAPTER 46: GUARDIANS' Promise**

The village of Ravenswood continued to bask in the afterglow of our wedding, and the sense of unity and joy remained palpable. The bonds we had forged, both old and new, were stronger than ever, and the legacy of the Guardians continued to inspire and guide us. As the crisp days of autumn settled in, we looked forward to the future with excitement and hope.

One morning, as the leaves rustled gently in the breeze and the sunlight filtered through the trees, Daniel and I gathered with the council to discuss the next steps for our community. The council chamber was filled with an air of anticipation, and the faces of the council members reflected their dedication and determination.

"Olivia, Daniel," Clara began, her voice steady and authoritative, "our recent discoveries have provided us with invaluable insights into the early teachings of the Guardians. We now have a deeper understanding of their commitment to balance, harmony, and wisdom. However, there is still much more to learn. We need to continue our exploration and ensure that we preserve this knowledge for future generations."

Lucas nodded in agreement. "The symbols and inscriptions we've found are a treasure trove of knowledge. We must study them carefully and use that knowledge to guide our efforts in the present and future."

Elara, ever the strategist, added, "We should also focus on sharing our discoveries with neighboring communities. The knowledge we've gained can help others strengthen their defenses and protect their worlds."

Alaric, his presence radiating confidence, said, "I'll oversee the preservation efforts and ensure that the ruins remain intact. We cannot afford to make any mistakes."

Daniel, standing beside me, placed a reassuring hand on my shoulder. "We'll face this together, Olivia. Our bond is our strength, and we can overcome any challenge."

I took a deep breath, feeling the weight of the responsibility before us. "Let's do this. We'll continue to uncover the secrets of the past and use that knowledge to build a future filled with hope and promise."

IN THE DAYS THAT FOLLOWED, the village of Ravenswood was a hive of activity. The council of Guardians and our team of researchers worked tirelessly to document and study the symbols and inscriptions found in the ancient ruins. The sense of unity and collaboration was strong, and it filled us with hope for the future.

Clara's expertise in ancient languages and symbols proved invaluable as she continued to translate the inscriptions. "These carvings speak of the early Guardians' commitment to unity and compassion. Their teachings emphasize the importance of working together and supporting one another."

Lucas nodded in agreement. "The artifacts we've found here also suggest that the early Guardians valued both magic and practical knowledge. They sought to use their abilities to protect and nurture their communities."

Elara's strategic mind helped us plan our excavation and preservation efforts. "We need to be thorough and methodical in our approach. Each discovery could provide valuable insights into the history and wisdom of the Guardians."

Alaric's leadership ensured that our efforts were carried out with care and precision. "We'll take every precaution to preserve the integrity of the ruins. This place is a testament to the strength and wisdom of the Guardians, and we must honor and protect it."

AS WE CONTINUED OUR research and exploration, we uncovered more about the history of the Guardians and their early teachings. The sense of connection to the past was profound, and it filled us with a renewed sense of purpose and determination.

One evening, as the sun set and cast a warm golden light over the ancient ruins, Daniel and I found a moment of quiet reflection. We stood in the clearing, gazing at the weathered stones and the intricate carvings that told the story of our ancestors.

"Olivia," Daniel said softly, "this place is a testament to the strength and wisdom of the Guardians. Their legacy continues to guide us, and it's our responsibility to honor and preserve it."

I smiled, feeling a deep sense of pride and gratitude. "Thank you, Daniel. Our bond and our connection to the Guardians have been our greatest strengths. Together, we can continue to protect our world and build a future filled with hope and promise."

He took my hand, his touch warm and reassuring. "We'll continue to uncover the secrets of the past and use that knowledge to guide us into the future. The light of the Guardians will continue to illuminate our path, just as it always has."

AS THE WEEKS TURNED into months, our efforts to uncover the secrets of the ancient ruins continued. The knowledge we gained provided valuable insights into the early teachings of the Guardians and guided our efforts to create a harmonious and just society.

One evening, as the sun set and cast a warm golden light over the village, we gathered in the town square to celebrate the Festival of Unity. The air was filled with the sounds of laughter and music, and the scent of delicious food wafted through the streets. The festival was a time to reflect on our journey, celebrate our achievements, and look forward to the future.

As I stood on the stage, addressing the gathered crowd, I felt a deep sense of pride and gratitude. "Tonight, we celebrate the unity and strength that have brought us here. We have faced darkness and emerged stronger. Our communities are thriving, and the legacy of the Guardians continues to guide us."

The crowd erupted in cheers, their faces filled with joy and hope. The sense of camaraderie and mutual support was palpable, and I could see the strength and resilience of our people shining through.

Daniel, Clara, Lucas, Elara, and Alaric joined me on the stage, their presence a testament to the bonds we had forged and the journey we had undertaken. Together, we looked out at the faces of our friends and allies, our hearts filled with hope and determination.

AS THE FESTIVAL CONTINUED, I found a moment of quiet reflection, standing at the edge of the village and gazing up at the stars. The night was clear, and the constellations seemed to twinkle with a gentle, comforting light. I felt the presence of the Guardians, their wisdom and strength a constant guide.

Daniel joined me, his presence a comforting balm to my soul. "Olivia, you have been our guiding light. Your strength and determination have inspired us all. Together, we will continue to build a future filled with hope and promise."

I smiled, feeling a deep sense of pride and gratitude. "Thank you, Daniel. Our bond has been our greatest strength. Together, we can face anything."

He took my hand, his touch warm and reassuring. "Our journey is far from over, but I know that we can handle whatever comes next. The light of the Guardians will continue to guide us, illuminating the path to a brighter tomorrow."

As we stood together, the gentle light of the stars casting a soothing glow over the village, I made a silent vow. We would continue to protect our world, no matter the cost. With the strength and resilience of our community, and the deepening bond between us, we would face whatever challenges lay ahead and build a future filled with promise and possibility.

The legacy of the Guardians would continue to shine, guiding us through the darkness and illuminating the path to a brighter tomorrow. And together, we would build a world filled with hope, unity, and endless possibilities.

### **CHAPTER 47: GUARDIANS' Future**

The crisp autumn air carried with it a sense of renewal and anticipation. The village of Ravenswood was alive with activity, and the legacy of the Guardians continued to inspire and guide us. The bonds we had forged, both old and new, were stronger than ever, and our community thrived under the unity and strength that had brought us through countless challenges.

One morning, as the sunlight filtered through the colorful leaves and cast a warm glow over the village, Daniel and I met with the council to discuss our progress and the exciting future that lay ahead. The council chamber was filled with an air of anticipation, and the faces of the council members reflected their dedication and determination.

"Olivia, Daniel," Clara began, her voice steady and authoritative, "our recent efforts have provided us with invaluable insights into the early teachings of the Guardians. We now have a deeper understanding of their commitment to balance, harmony, and wisdom. However, there is still much more to learn. We need to continue our exploration and ensure that we preserve this knowledge for future generations."

Lucas nodded in agreement. "The symbols and inscriptions we've found are a treasure trove of knowledge. We must study them carefully and use that knowledge to guide our efforts in the present and future."

Elara, ever the strategist, added, "We should also focus on sharing our discoveries with neighboring communities. The knowledge we've gained can help others strengthen their defenses and protect their worlds."

Alaric, his presence radiating confidence, said, "I'll oversee the preservation efforts and ensure that the ruins remain intact. We cannot afford to make any mistakes."

Daniel, standing beside me, placed a reassuring hand on my shoulder. "We'll face this together, Olivia. Our bond is our strength, and we can overcome any challenge."

I took a deep breath, feeling the weight of the responsibility before us. "Let's do this. We'll continue to uncover the secrets of the past and use that knowledge to build a future filled with hope and promise."

IN THE DAYS THAT FOLLOWED, the village of Ravenswood was a hive of activity. The council of Guardians and our team of researchers worked tirelessly to document and study the symbols and inscriptions found in the ancient ruins. The sense of unity and collaboration was strong, and it filled us with hope for the future.

Clara's expertise in ancient languages and symbols proved invaluable as she continued to translate the inscriptions. "These carvings speak of the early Guardians' commitment to unity and compassion. Their teachings emphasize the importance of working together and supporting one another."

Lucas nodded in agreement. "The artifacts we've found here also suggest that the early Guardians valued both magic and practical knowledge. They sought to use their abilities to protect and nurture their communities."

Elara's strategic mind helped us plan our excavation and preservation efforts. "We need to be thorough and methodical in our approach. Each discovery could provide valuable insights into the history and wisdom of the Guardians."

Alaric's leadership ensured that our efforts were carried out with care and precision. "We'll take every precaution to preserve the integrity of the ruins. This place is a testament to the strength and wisdom of the Guardians, and we must honor and protect it."

AS WE CONTINUED OUR research and exploration, we uncovered more about the history of the Guardians and their early teachings. The sense of connection to the past was profound, and it filled us with a renewed sense of purpose and determination.

One evening, as the sun set and cast a warm golden light over the ancient ruins, Daniel and I found a moment of quiet reflection. We stood in the clearing, gazing at the weathered stones and the intricate carvings that told the story of our ancestors.

"Olivia," Daniel said softly, "this place is a testament to the strength and wisdom of the Guardians. Their legacy continues to guide us, and it's our responsibility to honor and preserve it."

I smiled, feeling a deep sense of pride and gratitude. "Thank you, Daniel. Our bond and our connection to the Guardians have been our greatest strengths. Together, we can continue to protect our world and build a future filled with hope and promise."

He took my hand, his touch warm and reassuring. "We'll continue to uncover the secrets of the past and use that knowledge to guide us into the future. The light of the Guardians will continue to illuminate our path, just as it always has."

AS THE WEEKS TURNED into months, our efforts to uncover the secrets of the ancient ruins continued. The knowledge we gained provided valuable insights into the early teachings of the Guardians and guided our efforts to create a harmonious and just society.

One evening, as the sun set and cast a warm golden light over the village, we gathered in the town square to celebrate the Festival of Renewal. The air was filled with the sounds of laughter and music, and the scent of delicious food wafted through the streets. The festival was a time to reflect on our journey, celebrate our achievements, and look forward to the future.

As I stood on the stage, addressing the gathered crowd, I felt a deep sense of pride and gratitude. "Tonight, we celebrate the renewal and strength that have brought us here. We have faced darkness and emerged stronger. Our communities are thriving, and the legacy of the Guardians continues to guide us."

The crowd erupted in cheers, their faces filled with joy and hope. The sense of camaraderie and mutual support was palpable, and I could see the strength and resilience of our people shining through.

Daniel, Clara, Lucas, Elara, and Alaric joined me on the stage, their presence a testament to the bonds we had forged and the journey we had undertaken. Together, we looked out at the faces of our friends and allies, our hearts filled with hope and determination.

AS THE FESTIVAL CONTINUED, I found a moment of quiet reflection, standing at the edge of the village and gazing up at the stars. The night was clear, and the constellations seemed to twinkle with a gentle, comforting light. I felt the presence of the Guardians, their wisdom and strength a constant guide.

Daniel joined me, his presence a comforting balm to my soul. "Olivia, you have been our guiding light. Your strength and determination have inspired us all. Together, we will continue to build a future filled with hope and promise."

I smiled, feeling a deep sense of pride and gratitude. "Thank you, Daniel. Our bond has been our greatest strength. Together, we can face anything."

He took my hand, his touch warm and reassuring. "Our journey is far from over, but I know that we can handle whatever comes next. The light of the Guardians will continue to guide us, illuminating the path to a brighter tomorrow."

As we stood together, the gentle light of the stars casting a soothing glow over the village, I made a silent vow. We would continue to protect our world, no matter the cost. With the strength and resilience of our community, and the deepening bond between us, we would face whatever challenges lay ahead and build a future filled with promise and possibility.

The legacy of the Guardians would continue to shine, guiding us through the darkness and illuminating the path to a brighter tomorrow. And together, we would build a world filled with hope, unity, and endless possibilities.

### **CHAPTER 48: GUARDIANS' Legacy Unfolds**

As the autumn leaves continued to fall, the village of Ravenswood was filled with a sense of renewal and anticipation. Our efforts to uncover the secrets of the ancient ruins had deepened our understanding of the Guardians' teachings, and the unity and strength of our community had never been stronger. We were determined to honor the legacy of the Guardians and build a future filled with hope and promise.

One morning, as the crisp air carried the scent of pine and the sunlight filtered through the trees, Daniel and I gathered with the council to discuss our progress and the exciting future that lay ahead. The council chamber was filled with an air of anticipation, and the faces of the council members reflected their dedication and determination.

"Olivia, Daniel," Clara began, her voice steady and authoritative, "our recent efforts have provided us with invaluable insights into the early teachings of the Guardians. We now have a deeper understanding of their commitment to balance, harmony, and wisdom. However, there is still much more to learn. We need to continue our exploration and ensure that we preserve this knowledge for future generations."

Lucas nodded in agreement. "The symbols and inscriptions we've found are a treasure trove of knowledge. We must study them carefully and use that knowledge to guide our efforts in the present and future."

Elara, ever the strategist, added, "We should also focus on sharing our discoveries with neighboring communities. The knowledge we've gained can help others strengthen their defenses and protect their worlds."

Alaric, his presence radiating confidence, said, "I'll oversee the preservation efforts and ensure that the ruins remain intact. We cannot afford to make any mistakes."

Daniel, standing beside me, placed a reassuring hand on my shoulder. "We'll face this together, Olivia. Our bond is our strength, and we can overcome any challenge."

I took a deep breath, feeling the weight of the responsibility before us. "Let's do this. We'll continue to uncover the secrets of the past and use that knowledge to build a future filled with hope and promise."

IN THE DAYS THAT FOLLOWED, the village of Ravenswood was a hive of activity. The council of Guardians and our team of researchers worked tirelessly to document and study the symbols and inscriptions found in the ancient ruins. The sense of unity and collaboration was strong, and it filled us with hope for the future.

Clara's expertise in ancient languages and symbols proved invaluable as she continued to translate the inscriptions. "These carvings speak of the early Guardians' commitment to unity and compassion. Their teachings emphasize the importance of working together and supporting one another."

Lucas nodded in agreement. "The artifacts we've found here also suggest that the early Guardians valued both magic and practical knowledge. They sought to use their abilities to protect and nurture their communities."

Elara's strategic mind helped us plan our excavation and preservation efforts. "We need to be thorough and methodical in our approach. Each discovery could provide valuable insights into the history and wisdom of the Guardians."

Alaric's leadership ensured that our efforts were carried out with care and precision. "We'll take every precaution to preserve the integrity of the ruins. This place is a testament to the strength and wisdom of the Guardians, and we must honor and protect it."

AS WE CONTINUED OUR research and exploration, we uncovered more about the history of the Guardians and their early teachings. The sense of connection to the past was profound, and it filled us with a renewed sense of purpose and determination.

One evening, as the sun set and cast a warm golden light over the ancient ruins, Daniel and I found a moment of quiet reflection. We stood in the clearing, gazing at the weathered stones and the intricate carvings that told the story of our ancestors.

"Olivia," Daniel said softly, "this place is a testament to the strength and wisdom of the Guardians. Their legacy continues to guide us, and it's our responsibility to honor and preserve it."

I smiled, feeling a deep sense of pride and gratitude. "Thank you, Daniel. Our bond and our connection to the Guardians have been our greatest strengths. Together, we can continue to protect our world and build a future filled with hope and promise."

He took my hand, his touch warm and reassuring. "We'll continue to uncover the secrets of the past and use that knowledge to guide us into the future. The light of the Guardians will continue to illuminate our path, just as it always has."

AS THE WEEKS TURNED into months, our efforts to uncover the secrets of the ancient ruins continued. The knowledge we gained provided valuable insights into the early teachings of the Guardians and guided our efforts to create a harmonious and just society.

One evening, as the sun set and cast a warm golden light over the village, we gathered in the town square to celebrate the Festival of Unity. The air was filled with the sounds of laughter and music, and the scent of delicious food wafted through the streets. The festival was a time to reflect on our journey, celebrate our achievements, and look forward to the future.

As I stood on the stage, addressing the gathered crowd, I felt a deep sense of pride and gratitude. "Tonight, we celebrate the unity and strength that have brought us here. We have faced darkness and emerged stronger. Our communities are thriving, and the legacy of the Guardians continues to guide us."

The crowd erupted in cheers, their faces filled with joy and hope. The sense of camaraderie and mutual support was palpable, and I could see the strength and resilience of our people shining through.

Daniel, Clara, Lucas, Elara, and Alaric joined me on the stage, their presence a testament to the bonds we had forged and the journey we had undertaken. Together, we looked out at the faces of our friends and allies, our hearts filled with hope and determination.

AS THE FESTIVAL CONTINUED, I found a moment of quiet reflection, standing at the edge of the village and gazing up at the stars. The night was clear, and the constellations seemed to twinkle with a gentle, comforting light. I felt the presence of the Guardians, their wisdom and strength a constant guide.

Daniel joined me, his presence a comforting balm to my soul. "Olivia, you have been our guiding light. Your strength and determination have inspired us all. Together, we will continue to build a future filled with hope and promise."

I smiled, feeling a deep sense of pride and gratitude. "Thank you, Daniel. Our bond has been our greatest strength. Together, we can face anything."

He took my hand, his touch warm and reassuring. "Our journey is far from over, but I know that we can handle whatever comes next. The light of the Guardians will continue to guide us, illuminating the path to a brighter tomorrow."

As we stood together, the gentle light of the stars casting a soothing glow over the village, I made a silent vow. We would continue to protect our world, no matter the cost. With the strength and resilience of our community, and the deepening bond between us, we would face whatever challenges lay ahead and build a future filled with promise and possibility.

The legacy of the Guardians would continue to shine, guiding us through the darkness and illuminating the path to a brighter tomorrow. And together, we would build a world filled with hope, unity, and endless possibilities.

### **CHAPTER 49: GUARDIANS' Endeavor**

The crisp air of late autumn whispered through the village of Ravenswood, bringing with it the promise of new discoveries and the anticipation of the first snowfall. The trees, now bare, stood tall against the clear sky, their branches etched in intricate patterns. Our community remained resilient and united, driven by a shared purpose to honor the legacy of the Guardians and build a future filled with hope and promise.

One morning, as the village buzzed with activity and the fields lay in a serene, post-harvest calm, Daniel and I gathered with the council to discuss our progress and the plans for the coming months. The council chamber was filled with an air of determination, and the faces of the council members reflected their unwavering dedication.

"Olivia, Daniel," Clara began, her voice filled with resolve, "our recent efforts have brought us closer to understanding the early teachings of the Guardians. We now have a clearer picture of their commitment to balance, harmony, and wisdom. However, our work is far from over. We need to continue our exploration and ensure that we preserve this knowledge for future generations."

Lucas nodded thoughtfully. "The symbols and inscriptions we've found are invaluable. We must delve deeper into their meanings and use that knowledge to guide our efforts in the present and future."

Elara, ever the strategist, added, "We should also strengthen our alliances with neighboring communities. Sharing our discoveries can help others protect their worlds and create a network of support and collaboration."

Alaric, his presence radiating confidence, said, "I'll oversee the preservation efforts and ensure that the ruins remain intact. We must handle this with the utmost care and precision."

Daniel, standing beside me, placed a reassuring hand on my shoulder. "We'll face this together, Olivia. Our bond is our strength, and we can overcome any challenge."

I took a deep breath, feeling the weight of the responsibility before us. "Let's move forward with determination. We'll continue to uncover the secrets of the past and use that knowledge to build a future filled with hope and promise."

IN THE DAYS THAT FOLLOWED, the village of Ravenswood was a hive of activity. The council of Guardians and our team of researchers worked tirelessly to document and study the symbols and inscriptions found in the ancient ruins. The sense of unity and collaboration was palpable, and it filled us with hope for the future.

Clara's expertise in ancient languages and symbols proved invaluable as she continued to translate the inscriptions. "These carvings speak of the early Guardians' dedication to unity and compassion. Their teachings emphasize the importance of working together and supporting one another."

Lucas nodded in agreement. "The artifacts we've found here also suggest that the early Guardians valued both magic and practical knowledge. They sought to use their abilities to protect and nurture their communities."

Elara's strategic mind helped us plan our excavation and preservation efforts. "We need to be thorough and methodical in our approach. Each discovery could provide valuable insights into the history and wisdom of the Guardians."

Alaric's leadership ensured that our efforts were carried out with care and precision. "We'll take every precaution to preserve the integrity of the ruins. This place is a testament to the strength and wisdom of the Guardians, and we must honor and protect it."

AS WE CONTINUED OUR research and exploration, we uncovered more about the history of the Guardians and their early teachings. The sense of connection to the past was profound, and it filled us with a renewed sense of purpose and determination.

One evening, as the sun set and cast a warm golden light over the ancient ruins, Daniel and I found a moment of quiet reflection. We stood in the clearing, gazing at the weathered stones and the intricate carvings that told the story of our ancestors.

"Olivia," Daniel said softly, "this place is a testament to the strength and wisdom of the Guardians. Their legacy continues to guide us, and it's our responsibility to honor and preserve it."

I smiled, feeling a deep sense of pride and gratitude. "Thank you, Daniel. Our bond and our connection to the Guardians have been our greatest strengths. Together, we can continue to protect our world and build a future filled with hope and promise."

He took my hand, his touch warm and reassuring. "We'll continue to uncover the secrets of the past and use that knowledge to guide us into the future. The light of the Guardians will continue to illuminate our path, just as it always has."

AS THE WEEKS TURNED into months, our efforts to uncover the secrets of the ancient ruins continued. The knowledge we gained provided valuable insights into the early teachings of the Guardians and guided our efforts to create a harmonious and just society.

One evening, as the sun set and cast a warm golden light over the village, we gathered in the town square to celebrate the Festival of Unity. The air was filled with the sounds of laughter and music, and the scent of delicious food wafted through the streets. The festival was a time to reflect on our journey, celebrate our achievements, and look forward to the future.

As I stood on the stage, addressing the gathered crowd, I felt a deep sense of pride and gratitude. "Tonight, we celebrate the unity and strength that have brought us here. We have faced darkness and emerged stronger. Our communities are thriving, and the legacy of the Guardians continues to guide us."

The crowd erupted in cheers, their faces filled with joy and hope. The sense of camaraderie and mutual support was palpable, and I could see the strength and resilience of our people shining through.

Daniel, Clara, Lucas, Elara, and Alaric joined me on the stage, their presence a testament to the bonds we had forged and the journey we had undertaken. Together, we looked out at the faces of our friends and allies, our hearts filled with hope and determination.

AS THE FESTIVAL CONTINUED, I found a moment of quiet reflection, standing at the edge of the village and gazing up at the stars. The night was clear, and the constellations seemed to twinkle with a gentle, comforting light. I felt the presence of the Guardians, their wisdom and strength a constant guide.

Daniel joined me, his presence a comforting balm to my soul. "Olivia, you have been our guiding light. Your strength and determination have inspired us all. Together, we will continue to build a future filled with hope and promise."

I smiled, feeling a deep sense of pride and gratitude. "Thank you, Daniel. Our bond has been our greatest strength. Together, we can face anything."

He took my hand, his touch warm and reassuring. "Our journey is far from over, but I know that we can handle whatever comes next. The light of the Guardians will continue to guide us, illuminating the path to a brighter tomorrow."

As we stood together, the gentle light of the stars casting a soothing glow over the village, I made a silent vow. We would continue to protect our world, no matter the cost. With the strength and resilience of our community, and the deepening bond between us, we would face whatever challenges lay ahead and build a future filled with promise and possibility.

The legacy of the Guardians would continue to shine, guiding us through the darkness and illuminating the path to a brighter tomorrow. And together, we would build a world filled with hope, unity, and endless possibilities.

### **CHAPTER 50: ETERNAL Light**

The first snowfall of winter blanketed Ravenswood in a serene, white layer, transforming the village into a picturesque wonderland. The air was crisp and filled with the scent of pine, and the soft crunch of snow underfoot echoed the peacefulness of the season. Our community, unified and resilient, continued to thrive under the legacy of the Guardians, and the bonds we had forged were stronger than ever.

One clear morning, as the snow glistened in the sunlight and the village was alive with the joy of the season, Daniel and I gathered with the council for one final meeting to reflect on our journey and the path that lay ahead. The council chamber was filled with an air of accomplishment, and the faces of the council members reflected their pride and determination.

"Olivia, Daniel," Clara began, her voice warm and steady, "our journey to uncover the secrets of the Guardians has been nothing short of extraordinary. We have deepened our understanding of their teachings and strengthened our community. However, our work is never truly finished. We must continue to preserve this knowledge and pass it on to future generations."

Lucas nodded in agreement. "The symbols and inscriptions we've studied have provided us with invaluable insights. We must ensure that this wisdom is kept alive and used to guide our efforts moving forward."

Elara, ever the strategist, added, "We should continue to build alliances with neighboring communities. Sharing our knowledge can help others protect their worlds and create a network of support and collaboration."

Alaric, his presence radiating confidence, said, "I'll oversee the continued preservation efforts and ensure that the ruins remain intact. We must honor and protect this legacy with the utmost care."

Daniel, standing beside me, placed a reassuring hand on my shoulder. "We've come so far together, Olivia. Our bond is our strength, and we can face whatever challenges the future holds."

I took a deep breath, feeling the weight of our journey and the promise of the future. "Let's continue to move forward with hope and determination. We'll protect the legacy of the Guardians and build a future filled with endless possibilities."

IN THE DAYS THAT FOLLOWED, the village of Ravenswood continued to thrive. The council of Guardians and our team of researchers worked tirelessly to document and preserve the knowledge we had uncovered. The sense of unity and collaboration was stronger than ever, and it filled us with hope for the future.

Clara's expertise in ancient languages and symbols remained invaluable as she continued to translate and interpret the inscriptions. "These carvings speak of the Guardians' unwavering dedication to unity and compassion. Their teachings will continue to guide us."

Lucas nodded in agreement. "The artifacts we've found are a testament to the Guardians' wisdom. We must ensure that their teachings are passed on to future generations."

Elara's strategic mind helped us plan our ongoing preservation efforts. "We need to remain vigilant and thorough in our approach. Each discovery is a piece of the puzzle, and together, they form a complete picture of the Guardians' legacy."

Alaric's leadership ensured that our efforts were carried out with care and precision. "We'll take every precaution to protect the integrity of the ruins. This place is a beacon of hope and wisdom, and we must honor it."

AS WINTER DEEPENED, the village of Ravenswood was filled with the warmth of community and the spirit of celebration. The Festival of Light, a new tradition we had established to honor the Guardians, brought everyone together in joyous celebration. The village square was adorned with lanterns and decorations, and the air was filled with laughter and music.

As I stood on the stage, addressing the gathered crowd, I felt a deep sense of pride and gratitude. "Tonight, we celebrate the light that has guided us through darkness. We honor the legacy of the Guardians and the unity that has brought us here. Our communities are thriving, and we look forward to a future filled with hope and promise."

The crowd erupted in cheers, their faces illuminated by the soft glow of lanterns. The sense of camaraderie and mutual support was palpable, and I could see the strength and resilience of our people shining through.

Daniel, Clara, Lucas, Elara, and Alaric joined me on the stage, their presence a testament to the bonds we had forged and the journey we had undertaken. Together, we looked out at the faces of our friends and allies, our hearts filled with hope and determination.

AS THE FESTIVAL CONTINUED, I found a moment of quiet reflection, standing at the edge of the village and gazing up at the stars. The night was clear, and the constellations seemed to twinkle with a gentle, comforting light. I felt the presence of the Guardians, their wisdom and strength a constant guide.

Daniel joined me, his presence a comforting balm to my soul. "Olivia, you have been our guiding light. Your strength and determination have inspired us all. Together, we will continue to build a future filled with hope and promise."

I smiled, feeling a deep sense of pride and gratitude. "Thank you, Daniel. Our bond has been our greatest strength. Together, we can face anything."

He took my hand, his touch warm and reassuring. "Our journey is far from over, but I know that we can handle whatever comes next. The light of the Guardians will continue to guide us, illuminating the path to a brighter tomorrow."

As we stood together, the gentle light of the stars casting a soothing glow over the village, I made a silent vow. We would continue to protect our world, no matter the cost. With the strength and resilience of our community, and the deepening bond between us, we would face whatever challenges lay ahead and build a future filled with promise and possibility.

The legacy of the Guardians would continue to shine, guiding us through the darkness and illuminating the path to a brighter tomorrow. And together, we would build a world filled with hope, unity, and endless possibilities.

# About the Author

From a young age, I've been captivated by the magic of storytelling. I vividly remember the nights spent under the covers with a flashlight, devouring every book I could get my hands on. Those early encounters with words ignited a passion within me—a passion that only grew stronger as I did.

I started writing stories as soon as I could hold a pen, letting my imagination run wild on the pages of my notebooks. Each story was a new adventure, a fresh opportunity to explore different worlds and characters. My early works were raw and unpolished, but they were the foundation upon which I built my skills.

As I grew older, I dedicated myself to honing my craft. I immersed myself in literature, studying the works of great authors and learning from their techniques. I wrote consistently, always pushing myself to improve. I embraced feedback, seeing it as a valuable tool for growth rather than criticism. Through perseverance and passion, my writing began to evolve.

Now, after years of dedication and countless drafts, I'm proud to say that I've written my first four books. Each one is a testament to my journey, reflecting not only my growth as a writer but also my unwavering love for storytelling. These books are more than just stories; they are pieces of my heart and soul, crafted with care and creativity.

Writing is not just a hobby for me—it's a fundamental part of who I am. I look forward to continuing this journey, sharing my stories with the world, and connecting with readers who find joy and inspiration in my words.

Read more at https://www.tiktok.com/@strawberryshortcakevt48?_t=8rjNv4Uklyh&_r=

www.ingramcontent.com/pod-product-compliance
Lightning Source LLC
LaVergne TN
LVHW041218150826
845673LV00001B/444

* 9 7 9 8 2 3 0 0 6 3 3 3 9 *